HIDDEN!

by

Sandra Furuvald

www.hidden.sandrafuruvald.com

ISBN-13: 978-1468146257
ISBN-10: 1468146254

Library of Congress Control Number: 2012900110

Printed in the United States of America

HIDDEN!

by

Sandra Furuvald

Acknowledgements

Dedicated to Leanna for her inspiration.
Brittnie for her encouragement, and
Hilmar for his support

Table of Contents

FOREWORD

Michelle Nordahl moved to Southern California from Denver, Colorado at the age of fourteen. It was a tough age to be uprooted from her school, friends, and all that she called home. That was in 1980. They say time heals all wounds, but in Michelle's case it was, acceptance. She moved on and accepted the fact that Colorado was long gone and stepped into a different life with a desire to fit in. Eight years past and she was now a young lady, married with two children. Michelle had been through an extensive amount of abuse throughout her young life. She dubbed herself a survivor. What she didn't realize was the damage survival mode brought over the years of living there. She still hadn't acknowledged, nor was she aware of those repercussions.

As you read of her journey, don't be afraid to allow emotions to stir inside. This was the only way Michelle could get out of survival mode and into a new place where she could be used to bring others, and their future to fruition.

Don't allow fear to dictate your circumstances. Fear can de-rail you and put you on a course of self-destruction.

Challenge yourself to come outside your comfort zone. Just like Michelle, you know the truth in your heart, but prefer to live where you are most familiar. No longer give power to those debilitating people. No more excuses. As you read this book may strength and determination come over you to be who you were created to be.

Hidden!

PART I

CHAPTER 1

The Status Quo

An uneasy darkness fills my mind's eye. The entire atmosphere feels like some presence is pressing in around me. The cold resistance on my back is hard; perhaps I'm lying on a floor. The place is familiar, but from where? A long-ago memory of some dreadful event – something buried deep, deep into my subconscious is coming to the surface. Now the darkness is beginning to take form, becoming clearer.

This darkness is a person.

I didn't remember the half-mile stretch into my Southern California neighborhood tract, passing by the landscaped walkway lined with beautiful trees along a waterless bedrock brook. I couldn't remember turning right, then left, down the two shorter streets to my home. I couldn't remember how I got to this point. My mind was blank except for the awful vision that dominated my whole being. Then my mind came off auto-drive, and I recognized where I was and continued the drive home.

My visions had begun a few months ago. Every now and then a dark picture would flash in my mind.

I didn't know what it was, but I knew in my heart it was a picture of some kind of secret. A secret everyone knew but would not discuss.

As time passed, the pictures flashing forth began to dominate my day. Then they progressed into moving pictures, bursting forth at any moment. There was no controlling when they would appear.

Seeing visions were not an unusual occurrence for me. The meaning of the visions would eventually unfold. But this time the film in my mind was unclear and eerie.

I wanted to tell someone, but felt it was better to go it alone. What would I tell them? "I think I'm getting flashbacks from dropping too much acid years ago."

No, I'm not that person any more. A few years back my then boyfriend, Kris and I would party every weekend. Alcohol was his drug of choice and cocaine or anything else was mine. It's been over a year since I walked into that church, praying a prayer that reversed the course of my life. Kris doesn't realize – and may never grasp – how he saved my life.

A few years before I met Kris, there was a man named Adam. It was toward the end of my last attempt to graduate from high school. Alcohol and drugs, not school, were the predominant parts of my life. I met Adam while partying at a friend's house. It turned out he was my friend's roommate. There was something alluring about him. I found myself going to visit my friend quite often, knowing Adam would be there. Within a few weeks, Adam and I began to have long conversations, and I no longer needed an excuse to see him.

After a month, we were inseparable. We didn't want to be anywhere except with each other. I didn't realize the relationship was getting serious. I was young and having fun hanging out with this cute guy, drinking and taking whatever speed anyone had to offer. The term "boyfriend" wasn't one I used when I talked about Adam with my friends.

When he said he wanted me to meet his parents, it completely blindsided me. From that moment, I felt like I was on a fast-moving train with no stops until our final destination. Unfortunately, until then, I hadn't been aware of even boarding the train.

To get to Adam's parents' home, we drove for hours. It didn't occur to me to ask where they lived, but it became obvious it wasn't in the next city. Looking back, it seems ludicrous that I would allow someone I'd only known for a month to take me someplace I'd never heard of to meet people I wasn't sure I wanted to meet. In my drug-addled mind, however, I was on an adventure. As we neared our destination and turned off the main road, the surroundings became thick with trees. It was mesmerizing as our pace slowed through the forest and we came upon a still, glasslike lake. The overcast morning completed the enchanted moment. We continued until we came upon a lone trailer that seemed to be parked randomly in the middle of the forest.

As I scanned the area, it appeared we were in some sort of campground. When I was young, my family traveled by motor home all over the United States and stayed in various campgrounds. But it soon became apparent that Adam's parents were not on vacation.

I was familiar with the concept but unfamiliar with the reality that someone would choose to live in such a remote area. Where did they work? Shop? Who else did they communicate with? There was nothing around for miles, nor were there many other trailers. It was fall and very cold, a time of year most people didn't go camping.

I should have realized that being with Adam was a bad idea when I met his parents, and they were drinking screwdrivers at 7a.m. Vodka and orange juice for breakfast was radical even for me.

As Adam and I got deeper into drugs, every weekend ended up being a reason to get drunk, either with friends or just each other. I knew now there was no getting off this train, and I began to rationalize staying on board.

In Adam I saw a responsible person with a kind heart. He was a loyal employee and a hard worker. But on weekends, he became someone else.

His parents finally came out of hiding and moved into a condo in a remote city called Norco where Adam grew up. Looking back, I never felt right with him. And that became even more the case when I picked him up one day at his parents' home and found his mom sitting at the counter with a nice big black eye, drinking her morning screwdriver. I had no idea what was happening in this family, but I felt very uncomfortable when I saw that black eye.

As long as I can remember, I have known things about people or situations without anyone telling me. I somehow knew details about the lives of people I'd never met. I could practically predict when and how events would happen to people. My friends would ask me for advice about certain situations, and sometimes my advice would run counter to what they were planning to do. I would explain in detail what would happen should they choose to continue down a certain path. Every time someone went against my advice, the exact thing I predicted occurred.

Today I call this instinct or intuition "my gift." On this morning, however, my gift was still undeveloped. It rose from within and told me not to ask, "What happened?" What was very strange, and significant, was that no one else asked either. No concern was expressed for Adam's mom. It was as if I were the only one in the room who even noticed the obvious.

Yet I was oblivious to the gravity of the situation. I remember thinking, "Something's not right here," but I couldn't put my finger on it. Though my gift was not yet mature, on that day it was telling me to leave, lay down my feelings for Adam and never turn back.

In time I did leave, but only for a few months, and was drawn back to this peculiar family. Clearly, naïve! I didn't realize when I saw Adam's mother with the black eye that his dad was responsible. Or did I? The gift within may have been shouting loudly and clearly, but I didn't want to hear it. I had never before seen the results of a woman being beaten, and I sure didn't want to believe her husband did it. Adam's dad? I continued to rationalize other possibilities.

Adam and I regularly visited his brother Joe, his wife Cassie, and their baby boy, Joe Jr. They had a nice little apartment close to Adam's grandparents. Joe had a good job, and Cassie was a stay-at-home mom. But despite the perfect little façade, Cassie always seemed sad.

One day when Adam and Joe went to pick up some beer, she told me why: Joe was no different than his dad. Though Cassie didn't come right out and say it, she was warning me to get out before it was too late. I heard what she was saying, but I did not understand the terror behind her words. This was unknown territory for me.

How could a man become so angry and so full of hate and rage that he not only hit his wife but beat her so badly it left bruises?

How could two people continue to live in such a cesspool of disgust?

Cassie was screaming at me with her eyes to get out and get out now! The gift within urged me to run. In hindsight, I could have avoided a lot of turmoil and grief had I listened, but I just could not wrap my head around it.

Then it happened.

I suppose to anyone looking in from the outside, it was painfully obvious that it was only a matter of time before I was next. Adam and I were on one of our drug and alcohol induced weekends. We fought often, as I thought most couples did, but he had never hit me. Why didn't I see it coming?

All I recall is suddenly it was happening, and there was no way out. My time for escape had come and gone. Perhaps it was the drugs and alcohol, but it seemed surreal.

As time passed, I thought I kept the secret well hidden. But I was in a state of unbelief, call it denial, call it what you want.

We were at my parents' house, and my brother asked me how I got a black eye.

Everyone else just pretended not to notice. (As I look at society now, this seems to be a constant, let's just pretend it's not happening), and even though I suspected I was bruised, I intentionally avoided confirming it. When I went to a mirror, there it was. My whole left eyelid was purple. My brother gave me a condescending look and called me an idiot. Everyone else pretended nothing had happened. Conversations came and went with no one expressing concern or a desire to help.

As I look back, that was probably one of the most disturbing moments of my life. My family, who was supposed to care for me and was clearly aware of my situation, chose to do nothing. I later recognized, their cowardliness was typical of how they dealt with difficult realities.

I almost found the courage and self-worth to get out. One night we'd gone with Adam's buddies from work to a bar, where we began arguing. I didn't know what led to the incident, but the blow to my head should have been the wakeup call – having been thrown through a glass sliding door on a previous occasion apparently wasn't enough to bring me to my senses.

Adam made sure no one ever saw us arguing. If our conversations began to get even a little heated, he would politely excuse us, and we would leave. That's what happened on this night.

We walked to my truck in silence. I wasn't about to let Adam drive while he was so angry and drunk, so I got behind the wheel and took off my high heels to drive. Suddenly everything seemed to be happening in slow motion. I turned the ignition, but before I could get out of the parking lot...WHAM! I looked over and one of my shoes was in his hand. He was beating me over the head with the heel.

Even with the alcohol in my system, the pain pulsated through my head. Blood squirted all over the ceiling of the truck, and my vision became blurry. I was suddenly very aware of the severity of the situation, and fear became my ally. With no time to think, my survival instinct told me to jump despite the fact the truck was moving. I leapt and miraculously stayed on my feet. Immediately, I turned and ran in the opposite direction as fast as my bare feet would carry me. I found a deep ravine, slid down it and hid.

Adam must have acted fast and jumped into the driver's seat because I could hear the truck accelerate. He was looking for me. I didn't know if he saw the direction I headed, but I heard the sound of the engine getting closer and could see the headlights shining in my direction. I heard him shouting "Michelle, Michelle" as he drove back and forth through the parking lot. I dreaded the sound of the engine shutting off, as this would mean Adam was looking for me on foot.

Finally, to my relief, I heard the truck drive away. I didn't care that he took the truck or if I ever got it back. I waited at least fifteen minutes in that cold, wet, ravine to make sure he wasn't trying to trick me into giving up my hiding place.

"Now what, Michelle? It's one o'clock in the morning. You have no shoes, no phone, and no money." Then I remembered Jesse, Adam's friend from work, lived just around the corner. He and his roommates were good guys, and my gift told me he had a secret crush on me. They were all at the bar earlier that evening, and I could tell they weren't fooled by our leaving. They knew Adam and I were not getting along.

As I picked myself up, I was chilled and felt the rough concrete on my bare feet. California can get pretty cold in the winter. I kept an eye out for my truck in case Adam was still driving around searching for me. At Jesse's house, the lights were on. Thank God! They were still up.

I gave a hesitant knock, and Jesse opened the door with a guarded look. I wasn't sure if he was shocked to see me alone or whether the dried blood on my face caused him to be apprehensive. As I stepped through the doorway, it felt like I entered a wonderland. Finally a refuge; finally someone I could trust. I didn't get into details, just the basics: Adam and I had a fight, and he beat the crap out of me.

The guys offered to let me get cleaned up and stay the night. Jesse showed me the way down the stairs, through his bedroom and into the bathroom. I looked at myself in the mirror. My feet were filthy; my cute skinny jeans and blouse were tattered and dirty from hiding in the ravine. With the mixture of dirt and blood smeared on my face and my tangled, wild hair, I looked like a little lost orphan. Now I understood the look on Jesse's face when he opened the door.

I parted my long brown hair where I had taken the blows to my head, but the hair and blood were too clumped for me to see if I needed stitches. I pulled off my clothes. The hot shower felt soothing except for the stinging from the open wounds in my head. For at least fifteen minutes, I stood under the water, tears of embarrassment rolling down my face.

A knock on the door startled me. It was Jesse.

"Here's a clean shirt. I'll set it right here."

He not only gave me one of his shirts to wear but let me sleep in his bed. Although he slept in the same bed, I knew he had no intentions of any inappropriate actions, and that was, of course, correct. He was a real gentleman.

The next morning, while I was getting back into my dirty clothes, Jesse called me upstairs. My head was pounding, but I figured breakfast was beckoning so I went. When I got to the top of the stairs, Jesse and his two roommates stared with guilty sadness. I looked over at the open front door, and my heart dropped. My head began to spin, and I almost collapsed. I couldn't believe my eyes.

Adam and his grandfather were standing there. My first thought was, why would Jesse and his roommates do this? Why would they turn me over to the enemy? The grandfather motioned me to come with them. Both grandparents knew we women were being physically abused. They tried to help Adam's mom get away from his dad, but since his parents were alcoholics, the alcohol won.

As I walked out the door, his grandfather assured Jesse and the others I would be okay. I felt so ashamed. And yet I had to go. Or at least I thought I did. I was too blind to know that I had a choice and didn't have to leave with them. That would be the last time I saw those nice young men who befriended me when I really needed it.

The drive home was quiet. Grandpa lectured Adam about his behavior, but only for my benefit. I liked his grandparents. They were Christians. But I didn't understand why the grandmother gave up on her daughter who was married to a man who beat her.

Things settled down for a few weeks after that. Then the inevitable came – I was pregnant. I was happy, but I didn't think everyone else would share my enthusiasm. To my surprise, my parents, Adam's parents, and his grandparents all seemed fine. No one seemed to be bothered by it. Adam himself could not have cared less. I guess "apathetic" would be the most charitable way to describe his attitude.

Having a baby gave me a new focus, and I was hopeful that it would lead to an improved relationship with Adam. I was encouraged that his mother was getting help for her drinking, but I didn't realize that she couldn't quit while around a drunkard husband.

We no longer saw much of Adam's brother, which was sad because I became dear friends with his wife, Cassie. They moved, and their new home was over an hour away, which made it difficult to visit as often. Looking back, their move may have been subconsciously plotted, due to the fact their relationship was getting worse. Cassie wanted to have another baby, and Joe didn't. When I became pregnant, her desire intensified. She always wanted a girl to go along with her little boy. I found out I was having a girl, and within months, Cassie also was pregnant.

When Cassie had a little girl a few months after my Lisa was born, I was so happy for her. I thought maybe now we could find some joy in our lives.

But there was no joy in my situation other than my beautiful Lisa. She was now my life. In my heart, I vowed to escape the mess I was in.

###

Just when I thought I found a way out, both sets of parents and Adam's grandparents began discussing our getting married. I could not believe my ears.

My mom took me shopping for a simple wedding dress, and they decided we would all go to Las Vegas so we could get married in the same chapel my parents did. Of course, Adam assured me that he had changed and things would be different from now on.

I was in a state of shock. Why didn't anyone see the double life everyone in this family was leading? Why did I have to be a part of this? Why didn't I matter? Much to my dismay, no one could hear my thoughts.

After the brief wedding ceremony, my new husband went out drinking with his dad, and I went back to the hotel and cared for Lisa. Being with her was the only way to forget the nightmare I could not awaken from. Her bald little head, huge blue eyes, and precious chubby cheeks brought purpose to my life.

I was no longer surprised when Adam promised to change but never did. Trust had been broken a long time ago and could never be repaired. Every time he got angry, it was taken out on my face. The next two months were filled with sheer terror and threats. Not just to me this time but also to my family. I knew the threats were legitimate. He had two great teachers who stood behind him in whatever he threatened to do.

Adam broke my father's thumb, a message to me to stay put.

On one occasion, a neighbor must have heard us arguing and phoned the police. Once again, I believed I was finally rescued. I tried to leave, but my truck wouldn't start. Adam removed a coil to disable it. The police were kind and understanding. It was evident they were familiar with my type of situation and knew exactly what happened. They bought me a new part for my truck so I could leave.

Then Adam dropped a bomb. "You can leave, but Lisa stays." The police confirmed there was nothing they could do because she was his daughter, too.

This man was pure evil and knew just where my allegiance lay. There was no way I was going anywhere without my Lisa, so I stayed.

One night, when the rage began again, Adam threw me to the ground with Lisa in my arms. I was shocked that he had attacked me while I was holding her. She was a helpless baby, only four months old. What was he thinking? He could have hurt her.

I looked into Lisa's screaming little face and knew I had to disappear. I had to do it for her. I picked us up off the floor and vowed to myself, "Maybe me, but not her; not now, not ever."

###

In terror for my life and my daughter's life, I plotted my escape. I was so terrified that I imagined Adam could hear my thoughts, so I never thought of my plans while in his presence.

Eventually I somehow found the strength to leave. I confided in my supervisor at work. She was the first person to even hint at support other than Cassie. During the next few months, with the help of my supervisor, I summoned the courage to carry out my escape. I wanted to phone Cassie and tell her my plan, but for her own well-being, it was best she knew nothing.

I took a chance and asked my parents if they would help, and much to my surprise they agreed. They were not interested in knowing about the terror in which I lived; they just knew I didn't want to be in that home with Adam anymore, and that was enough.

On the days I got home from work before Adam, I would pack things in suitcases and hide them. Finally, the day came. My supervisor gave me the day off, knowing what I needed to do. My parents pulled up about thirty minutes after Adam left for work. He worked just ten minutes away, which made the situation that much more intense.

It took hours for us to load everything, and for every moment of that, I was afraid he would walk through the door. I knew if that happened, he literally would kill me. Either way it would be over, so I kept pressing forward. The thought of my death leaving him the privilege of raising Lisa, was like pure adrenaline pumped through my veins.

When we finally loaded the last of our belongings, I put my wedding ring on the kitchen counter and closed the door. Still in a panic, I buckled Lisa into her car seat, started the car, and pulled out of the driveway. I had done it! I had escaped!

Or had I?

The anticipated phone call that evening was petrifying. I wished I'd thought to take the phone off the hook. The phone ringing was like dreaded nails on a chalkboard. Adam wanted to know what was going on.

What was going on? I left, that's what was going on.

"How long are you going to stay with your parents?"

"I haven't thought about that."

"I understand you need a break. When are you coming back?"

"Are you serious? I'm not coming back."

His anger was palpable. I knew I had gone well beyond the safety zone. I could almost feel his fist coming through the phone, and I began to shake.

"I have to go, Adam."

"Where do you have to go?"

"I have to hang up now. Goodbye."

The next day I reluctantly went to work, leaving behind the safety of my parents' home and my precious Lisa. My only solace was the knowledge that Adam was a dedicated employee who would not miss work.

I made it through my job that first day. After work, I was free to go to my parents' home and not the prison where I previously lived, a thought that brought about an unfamiliar liveliness. Even the longer commute and additional traffic didn't bother me. I felt liberated.

That exhilaration ended as soon as I turned the corner to my parents' home and spotted Adam's car parked across the street. I kept my head straight, moving only my eyes to see if he was in the car. If he caught my eye, that would be an open invitation to approach me. Pretending not to see him, I pulled into the driveway and quickly got out of the car. Walking as fast as I could down the walkway, I nonetheless felt like I was in a slow-motion movie scene. I couldn't reach the door fast enough. At the same time, I didn't want to appear to be in a hurry and give away the fact I had seen him.

Finally, I got up the step and reached for the door handle to turn the knob. Click. Terror gripped my heart. It was locked! This couldn't be happening. I pulled my key ring from my purse, but I was shaking so hard I couldn't get the key in the lock. Time slowed down, and I feared my brief freedom was about to end.

Forcing my hand still, I unlocked the door and burst into the house quickly, closing the door and locking it behind me. To my relief, I heard voices in the kitchen. Adam never got out of the car. I threw my purse down and ran into the den and saw Lisa watching TV. The sight of her counteracted the terror inside. I picked her up and held her close.

"I love you so much, Lisa."

"I love you too, Mommy."

All I could do was smother her in kisses. Her giggles were music to my ears, slowing my heartbeat to a normal pace.

###

I was stunned the next evening when I came home and Adam was again parked in the same spot. But once more, he didn't get out of his car.

This continued for several nights. He would drive to my parents' home and sit outside, never leaving the car. I didn't know what he was up to, but I knew it wasn't good. I phoned the police after about a week of this behavior. Their response stunned me.

"We can't keep someone from parking across the street from your home, ma'am. I suggest you get a restraining order."

A few days later, on a Friday, I came home from work and Adam's car was not in its usual spot. I could not believe it. He must be parked somewhere else watching from a distance, I thought.

I drove around, but no, he wasn't there. A huge sigh of relief came over me as I pulled into the driveway. He gave up. I won! I was free!

Practically dancing into my parents' home, I instantly noticed something was wrong. Terror again gripped my heart. Lisa was nowhere to be found. I yelled for my mom.

"Where's Lisa?"

She came toward me and said matter-of-factly, "Her dad has her. He wanted to have her for the weekend."

"What?"

This was beyond my comprehension. Did she not know what would happen? Did she not understand that I might never see Lisa again?

"You let him in this house? You let him near her? You let him take her? What could you possibly be thinking?"

She explained that he should have her every other weekend just like all separated dads.

Was this really happening? Was my mom really that blind?

As my emotions began to stir, I felt like I was in a scene from the old television show, *The Twilight Zone*. In each episode, someone would fail to anticipate some weird, freakish thing that would land them in the twilight zone.

I called the police to help me get Lisa back, but once again there was nothing they could do because she was also Adam's child, and we were not divorced. Hanging up the phone in defeat, I believed I would never get her back.

Adam didn't want to spend the weekend with Lisa. He just wanted to torment me and was prepared to use her to do it. As the evening grew longer, I couldn't just sit around. I phoned some friends and went out and got drunk. Even so, it was the longest weekend I ever experienced. I felt petrified and helpless.

Sunday evening came, and I was at Adam's front door to pick up Lisa with a faint hope they would be there. Before I knocked, I took a deep breath. "Focus, Michelle. You're on a mission! Get in, get Lisa and leave without incident."

Adam opened the door, and I silently squeezed passed him. Lisa was playing on the floor. Without hesitation, I scooped her up, grabbed the bag my mom had packed, and headed for the door. Again, I knew if I made eye contact with Adam, he would take it as a challenge. As I headed for the door, he stepped in front of us and threatened me in that harsh tone I knew so well.

"You're not going anywhere."

Somehow I found my feet as they stepped around him and out the door. As the pace of my footsteps increased, my terror grew, but I didn't look back. I got us in the car, locked the doors, put Lisa in her car seat and got out of there as fast as I could. As I drove away, I allowed myself to exhale. I looked over and stared at the beauty sitting in her car seat next to me. Never, never, never would I ever again allow her to be in harm's way!

When I got to my parents' home, I explained to my mom that there would be no reason for her to ever let Adam back in the house, and under no circumstances should she let him take Lisa again. It was clear she was clueless about what I went through these past two years.

The next day after work, I went to see an attorney. She explained that Adam was entitled to joint custody and mapped out all the visitations he would have, including taking Lisa every other summer.

The lawyer's voice seemed to become thicker. My head began to spin as anxiety welled in my throat. I couldn't believe my ears. Did she not hear me? He's abusive; he's threatening me; he just came and took her. Doesn't any of this make you want to protect me and my child? According to the law, there was nothing I could do.

This was not acceptable. I left the attorney's office feeling once again that I had to scramble to survive. Why wouldn't anyone help me? The police, lawyers – hell, even my own mother - weren't willing to stick up for me. Wasn't anyone willing to protect me?

The answer was clear when I got home and found Adam sitting outside again. My heart beat faster, and my body shook. Lisa was with me this time. As I lifted her from her car seat, I could see out of the corner of my eye that Adam was still in his car. Could I beat him inside? I had to try.

My parents worked at night, so I was alone. I got my house key in hand, picked up Lisa and sprinted to the front door. At the door, I fumbled with the key. He was getting out of the car. I told myself, "Get the key in the lock." I could hear his car door close. The key went in, I flung open the door, slammed it shut, and turned the lock.

Against the door, I stood still, hearing only the heaviness of my breath. I listened for footsteps, but there were none. As I took off my coat, I heard a car door and figured he was back in his car. I began to relax a bit, picked up Lisa to get her a bottle, and turned right into Adam.

Again I was seized by terror. My heart was pounding with shock. I thought for sure I was having a heart attack. Then a strange thought occurred to me: "Don't let him see the fear; it will only empower him and disempower you."

Still in disbelief that he found a way into the house, I began talking to him in a calm manner disguising the panic within. It seemed inevitable that regardless whether I survived this encounter, Adam was going to take Lisa and I would never see her again. He knew the only way to get to me was through her.

Adam took the phone off the hook, knowing I would call the police the first chance I got. He did not know, though, about the second phone line upstairs. By this time Lisa had fallen asleep in my arms. "Could I go upstairs and put Lisa to bed?" I asked him, as I fought to remain calm. "Then we can talk about the future."

Reluctantly he nodded. I walked upstairs and headed straight for the second phone line. Despite my panic and fear, I calmly dialed 911.

"911. What's your emergency?"

"My ex-husband broke into our home. My daughter and I are in danger."

That's when Adam reached around me and ripped the phone from my hand, throwing it against the wall.

He grabbed sleeping Lisa from my arms and ran with her. She was now wide awake and screamed as he thundered down the stairs with me scrambling behind them. I knew he was a monster but wasn't quite sure how crazy he was. I soon found out when I caught up to them in the backyard. He was holding Lisa over the pool by one arm threatening to drop her.

"Why did you call the police? Why did you have to do that?"

"I was scared. I didn't know what to do. I didn't know why you were here."

"Why I was here? I'm here to take you two home. Now you're going to have them put me in jail."

"No, no, I won't. I promise."

"I'm going to drop her if you don't leave with me right now before they get here."

As Lisa yelled, all I could think of was getting her back in my arms. Then for no understandable reason, he broke down and gave her back to me. At that moment, I heard the glorious sound of sirens as they came to our rescue.

"I promise I will leave you alone; please don't have them arrest me."

"I won't. I promise. It will be all right."

Adam slowly moved toward me. "I don't believe you."

"It will be fine Adam. I will tell them it was a mistake and we will go home." Immediately, there was a shout from the door.

"Huntington Beach PD."

I ran to the door and explained what happened, and included his life-threatening stunt with Lisa. When all was said and done, much to my shock they walked him to his truck and told him never to come back.

"That's it? No jail time? Nothing?"

"My advice is to get a restraining order," said one of the officers. "There's nothing else we can do without it."

I could not believe my eyes and ears. I thought I was in a different dimension and wasn't hearing correctly. I brought myself back to the present time and place, and reality hit me. With Adam free, I had no protection; no safety; I was dead!

But I was wrong. Adam did not return.

CHAPTER 2

Free at Last

I didn't know it at the time, but God was intervening. He was my protection. He was my safety. He had a plan for my life.

Days turned into months, and before I knew it, Lisa was about to turn two years old. I was now working at a trucking company.

My job required me to be in the office, but through the large window, I had a view of the activity in the dispatch office as drivers came and went.

All the drivers had to check in with Frank, the dispatcher. Being pals with Frank gave me an opportunity to discreetly check out the handsome blond driver who had caught my eye.

"Frank, who's the blond surfer dude who has the Arizona route?" I asked one day.

"I don't know any surfer dudes, Michelle. The only two blonds I know are from Sweden."

"Sweden? Are you sure? He has blond hair to his shoulders. He totally looks like a surfer."

"Nope, that's Kris, and he's not a surfer. He's a Swede."

Being the nice guy he was, Frank mentioned my interest to Kris. The next thing I knew, Mr. Surfer Dude from Sweden walked into my office. His stunning features and quiet demeanor confounded my thinking.

He wasn't tall, about five-foot nine, but perfect for me as I was barely over five feet. He had a rugged face, stoic looking, with deep-set blue eyes and a smile that melted my heart.

"Hello, I'm Michelle," I managed to get out.

"Kris – with a K."

"Hello Kris with a K."

That was it. He turned and walked out of my office.

This was unusual behavior, but not knowing Swedes, I didn't know how to assess it. Nor did it really matter because he was so cute – strange but definitely cute! I felt like a high school girl experiencing her first crush.

Every night after that, Kris would come into my office after his shift and pull himself up on the desk across from mine without saying a word. I wasn't sure what to make of this and felt a bit nervous about being stared at while I was inputting data into the computer. To break the silence, I began asking him questions. He would say just enough to answer but never elaborate or respond with a question of his own. His shyness became quite apparent.

I figured there must be a reason he continued coming back. It took a few weeks, but I finally worked up the courage to ask, "Do you want to go out or what?"

I was caught by surprise when he said, with a shrug of his shoulders, "Sure," and walked out the door. That was it? "Sure?" Shouldn't we have set a day or time? "Sure?"

The next night he didn't show up at my office, instead he was waiting next to my truck when I got off work. For the first time in two weeks, he began the conversation.

"Are you ready?"

Hmm. I guess we are going on a date, and I guess it's now. Lisa was safe at home with my parents, and I had no other plans.

I gave him my own, "Sure."

He followed me to my house, and we took the tractor from his big rig to a beach with beautiful cliffs in a place called Corona Del Mar. We stayed up all night had a few wine coolers and great conversation. It was magical. As the sun rose over the horizon, he dropped me off at my parents' home. It was such an unforgettable time that I didn't want it to end. Perhaps it didn't have to.

"Do you want to come to a birthday party tonight?"

"Sure."

"Great! It starts at six. Now go home and get some rest."

He leaned into me and gave me a kiss goodbye. "See ya."

My heart melted.

That evening came, and I wasn't sure he would show. He drove his route all day the day before, then stayed up all night with me. I thought for sure he would be too exhausted and would cancel. It had been my experience that guys were pretty flaky. But when I saw him pull up, my heart skipped a beat.

"Whoa, Michelle, you barely know this guy."

I ran – then caught myself and slowed to a quick walk – to his car. He opened his door, and in his hand was a bouquet of flowers. Not only did he show up, he brought me flowers. My insides were in turmoil from his thoughtfulness, a kind of consideration I was far from used to.

As I watched him participate in Lisa's second birthday party, I couldn't help but be in awe of this amazing person who walked into my life. Most men would be cautious dating someone with a child but not Kris. It turned out he had a six-month-old boy named Steven who lived in Sweden with his ex-girlfriend.

After that first date, it seemed there was no stopping us.

One night Frank, the dispatcher, put a phone call through to me. Reluctantly, I answered. No one ever called me at work. When I heard the voice on the other end, the old terror surged through my veins and my body began to shake. I tried to stay calm, and listened as Adam asked to meet with me.

We had never gotten a divorce because I didn't want to give Adam any access to Lisa. The only way a divorce was going to happen would be if I got full custody and he had no visitation rights. I didn't care about child support. I just wanted him out of our lives. No lawyer or court was willing to give me that.

"Can we meet? I have the divorce papers, and they're drawn up the way you want them. I need you to sign them."

Was this some kind of trick? It seemed too good to be true.

"Okay, I will meet with you, but only at a restaurant. You are not to go to my parents' home under any circumstances."

"All right, I'll meet you at Bob's restaurant tomorrow around 5:30."

I couldn't believe Adam had found me. I felt a dark familiarity I couldn't shake. Just then Kris walked into my office. I jumped, still shaken by the phone call. Kris didn't know I was still married, and I wasn't sure how he would react.

But what else could I do? By now Kris meant a lot to me. I couldn't hide my past from him any longer, nor could I continue to hide from it.

I came clean and told him everything. To my absolute amazement, he seemed a little disappointed but glad I would soon be divorced. He agreed to go with me the next day. Once again, little did I know God was orchestrating this series of events.

The next day Kris and I were driving to my parents' home to drop off Lisa before heading to the restaurant when he pointed to the people in the car next to us.

"Do you know them? It looks like they're trying to get our attention."

I looked over and to my shock it was Adam. He was nowhere near the restaurant but on his way to my parents'. Why did I think anything might have changed? Why did I let myself trust that he would keep his word?

"Yep, that's Adam, my ex. I don't know who the other person is."

By the time we reached the house, I was so panic-stricken I couldn't get out of the truck. I locked the doors after Kris got out and sat paralyzed with fear, holding Lisa tight. I'm pretty sure Kris thought I was having a melt down.

After what seemed like 10 minutes, Kris was able to talk me out of the truck and assured me that nothing was going to happen to me or Lisa.

Reluctantly I opened the door, grabbed Lisa and rushed into the house. Once Lisa was safely inside, I was able to collect my thoughts and face my worst nightmare. With great hesitation, I walked to the driveway.

"What are you doing here, Adam? We had an agreement to meet at the restaurant."

"When I saw you, I didn't see any harm in following you to the house."

He didn't have a clue the trauma caused by that single act. Or maybe he did.

He handed me the divorce papers to sign.

As I began to read the two-page document, the woman with Adam began spouting off.

"You're going to regret not letting Lisa see her father."

Then she blurted out something that revealed to me how I and every other woman in an abusive relationship can be truly blinded by their lack of self-value. "He put me in the hospital, and I'm still with him."

Shocked by her statement, I looked at her and noticed my wedding ring on her finger. I looked at Adam and knew why they were in such a hurry to get the divorce papers signed. They had gotten married. He hadn't told her that he was still married, but she found out and here we were.

I went into the house and looked over the papers to make sure everything was as it should be. I didn't care about the money he was ordered by law to pay me. All I needed was to see that I had full custody of Lisa. As I read the document, I found it. It was there. He had no say-so in her life whatsoever. I signed.

Still distressed, I walked back outside to give him the papers and tell him to keep his money. Getting money from him meant contact, and I did not want that.

"Here they are and keep your money."

"Legally the child support had to be in there or they wouldn't finalize the divorce," Adam said. Then he thanked me, and they drove off.

Kris had been outside with them this whole time. As they drove off, he looked at me and saw the dread still on my face. He pulled me close to him, and all the terror from the past years fell from my body as I wept in his arms.

It was over. My living nightmare was finally over.

CHAPTER 3

The Learning Curve

During the next two years, Kris and I became very close, so close that I knew he was going to ask me to marry him. But I pushed him away. Something gnawed inside and kept telling me I didn't deserve this amazing person in my life. And yet I loved him so much I couldn't just walk away.

Kris told me stories about a church he used to attend when he lived in Southern California as a child, before he moved to Sweden. People would come to the church in wheelchairs and leave walking. Demon-possessed people would become free – the demon would actually come out of the person and that person would be changed in an instant.

I never heard of this kind of church or these miraculous healings. I had a vague notion of God, but that was it. I didn't know He was real and was down here on earth. It was hard to imagine He cared enough to actually talk to people, heal them, and set them free of demons. Ironically, demons were more real to me than God.

As the months passed, I would lie in bed and listen to Kris's stories. I discovered this church was the reason he returned to America. However, since his move to Sweden, the church changed locations and he couldn't find it. One day while driving his truck route for work, he happened to glance over and see a big sign with the church's name. Because he was on a deadline he couldn't search out the exact location. He did remember it was off of the 605 freeway. It became clear to me that finding this church was critical to Kris.

I worked off the 605 Freeway, so late one afternoon I decided to find the church for him. It would be a gift that would make him very happy and, perhaps, make me feel worthy of him. I got off at the only freeway exit I knew, Imperial Highway, and drove up and down the street without seeing it. I stopped at a pay phone and looked up the name of the church, Community Chapel. I didn't know there could be more than one church with the same name. The phone book listed the addresses, but none were on Imperial Highway. I then phoned each one, only to get an answering machine. This was frustrating because I knew it had to be nearby.

Disappointed, I began to make my way back to the freeway. As I sat at a red light before the freeway on-ramp, I dared to ask God if He were real.

"God if you're real, help me find this church."

At that moment a strange thing happened. I actually heard a thought in my head that was not my own. It said, "Make a right turn."

Without hesitation, I responded. To my amazement, on the right-hand side of the street was the church I had been searching for and the big sign that read "Community Chapel World Outreach." Absolutely thrilled with myself, I hurried to Kris's home and told him the story.

He was in church that next Sunday, though, unfortunately, I had to work and couldn't go with him. At work, I told a co-worker how Kris had looked for this church and how disappointed I was that I couldn't be there with him to share in the moment of his return. Hearing my disappointment, she told me about her church and invited me to attend the evening service with her after work.

As we walked into the church and headed straight to the front row, my co-worker introduced me to others. A few people sat on the floor in front of us, which I thought a bit odd but just assumed that was how they did things there. It was a simple church. A plain cross hung on the wall behind the stage. Where was Jesus, I wondered? Why wasn't He hanging on the cross? Where were the stained glass windows and the altar?

Then a band came in and sang songs about the love of Jesus and worshipping him. This was all completely strange to me. The only church I could remember was a Catholic church my family attended once in a while. This was no Catholic service for sure.

Next they took an offering, which seemed normal to me, but then the priest, or whatever he was, came out in a suit.

Another man made announcements, and he wore jeans and a t-shirt. Was I in a cult? They didn't even have on robes. Everyone sat down as the preacher guy began to speak. People had their Bibles and were eagerly following along in them. That was something else strange. How could they even follow what the guy was talking about? How could they understand what the Bible meant?

While wondering about all this, my attention was drawn to the people sitting on the floor in front of me. One guy was not facing forward or paying attention to the preacher.

Since everything else was strange to me, maybe this was something some of them did as well. I began to think it a bit awkward that he was staring at me. Wow! Did I stand out that much that he knew I was an outsider?

After a few more minutes, I began to feel very uncomfortable and wanted to leave. But I was sitting in the front row and everyone would see me walk out. I did not want to draw any more attention to myself. As my discomfort increased, I noticed that the guy on the floor staring at me was specifically looking at my legs. I had on a dress and white lace-looking nylons.

After awhile the husband of the couple I met earlier, who was sitting next to me, told the guy on the floor to turn around and face forward.

Now I knew this was not part of the service. The guy on the floor kept turning back around and staring at my legs. I could not hear a word the preacher was saying because I felt so dirty and awkward with this guy lusting over my legs. I sat there in disbelief.

Finally, the gentleman next to me took off his jacket and put it over my legs. That did it. Just like that, the man on the floor turned toward the preacher and never looked back. I sat through the rest of the service with the jacket covering my legs, filled with thanks for this man who came to my rescue.

After church, I thanked my friend for inviting me and headed home as fast as I could. I called Kris, anxious to hear how his day went. He told me he had a life-changing experience at his new church. He saw people he hadn't seen in years. He also re-dedicated his life to the Lord, though I wasn't sure what that meant.

I told him that I had gone to church, too, with a girlfriend from work. I didn't go into great detail about my experience but did tell him about the freak who kept staring at my legs. I decided that if that was what church was like there was no need to go back. Kris assured me there was something wrong with that guy and invited me the following week to Community Chapel.

In the coming week, he talked about getting baptized and about the singles group he wanted to become involved with. I was very happy for him but didn't have a clue what he was talking about. I remembered my parents telling me about being baptized as a baby. Why did he want to get baptized now? I never heard of adults being baptized. But I had to admit this was the most excited I'd ever seen him, and that warmed my heart.

Something good had happened to Kris – and yet he was somehow becoming distant.

The next Sunday morning I went to church with him. Again, the same type of setup as the previous church. It was very strange to me. Later I found out that non-Catholic churches don't have Jesus on the cross because they prefer to focus on His resurrection rather than His death. The church members were welcoming and friendly, and the church service was lively as well with a band and a choir. It was a surprise to have fun in church.

Afterward Kris introduced me to the people he met the previous week and to the co-pastors, a mother and daughter team. I did not realize how controversial that was at the time. The mother was very nice, and I told her I wanted what Kris had, to receive Jesus into my life. Before we left, she said a prayer with me.

Although I was very positive about the church, a strange thing occurred. To my surprise, each time Kris introduced me to someone, he referred to me as "my friend." It was quite awkward and seemed as if he were embarrassed by me.

Then that night when Kris and I went back to the evening service, he said something I thought was truly bizarre. "Ya know," he said, "we don't always have to sit together."

Now my gift was in full working order. I saw the future and knew we were going to be married, so none of this or what was to follow made any sense to me. One week we're together and the next week I'm not the girl for him, though he had not come right out and said that.

As the weeks went by, even though Kris didn't want others to see us as a couple, they did anyway. I guess it was obvious that we belonged together.

This was a very confusing time for me. I was excited about my growing involvement with the church and what I was learning about God and the spirit realm. But where was my relationship going with Kris?

We still talked on the phone, and I would go to his apartment. It was as if nothing had changed unless we were at church. There he became really distant, almost avoiding me.

By now Lisa was four years old, and I began taking her to kids' church, which she enjoyed. Kris and I joined the Bible College at Community Chapel and took a course called Catechism. One week we would study something from the Bible and the next week actually do what we had learned.

For example, we practiced foot-washing, in which some would sit while others washed their feet in a basin. At the time I didn't understand why we were doing this other than that Jesus had done it. I found it easier to wash the feet of others than to have my own feet washed, which was extremely humbling.

We learned why grown people got baptized and studied something about circumcision of the heart, which went right over my head.

What really excited me was the idea that someone being baptized came out of the water a new person and that the old person was gone. That sounded really good to me because I didn't much like myself, and it would be nice to become someone else. Kris and I eventually did get baptized. It was a wonderful experience, though I didn't quite feel the newness I was anticipating.

We attended small groups that discussed Bible lessons and participated in activities of the singles group. I seemed to be on a fast track in my new surroundings.

Although Kris acted like an acquaintance when we were at church events, I pretended it didn't bother me. I took what I could get. I loved him. Even though I was growing in my Christianity, I still lacked the self-esteem to confront Kris about his strange behavior toward me.

CHAPTER 4

Hanging Tough

I no longer had any desire to drink, do drugs or party, and I wasn't hanging out with my old friends from school. I tried to bring a few of them to church, but they weren't interested. They looked at me differently now.

For some reason I could not be their friend anymore. That was okay with me. I was making new friends at church and having a really good time.

Back then I didn't know the church frowned upon sex before marriage. One night at Kris's apartment I had to ask, "Are we supposed to be having sex?"

With what seemed to be sadness in his voice, he confirmed my suspicions. "No."

So that was it. That's why he was acting so strangely. We then tried to break off our relationship, but we couldn't stay away from each other.

One night after Bible College, I got in my car and heard God speak to me very clearly: "Don't worry about what you're about to see with Kris. I will take care of him."

This was startling. What did it mean?

I found out soon enough. The next Sunday there was a new girl in church, new to me anyway. Everyone else seemed to know her, though she hadn't been in church lately.

She approached Kris and me after church.

"Hi, I'm Jessica. What's your wife's name?"

Wow! That was bold. She was hitting on Kris thinking he has a wife.

"Oh, huh, this is Michelle. She's not my wife though, just a friend."

"I saw you ride up on your motorcycle. How 'bout a ride sometime?"

"Yeah. Definitely! Let me know when."

I could not believe my ears. This girl was totally after him, and he was buying into it.

"Awesome! We'll talk later. Bye. Bye, Michelle."

"Okay, bye. It was nice meeting you," I managed to mutter without sincerity.

I stood there speechless. I thought about what God said to me the night before. This

Jessica was a she-devil, and I knew it. Of course, Kris couldn't see a thing. Not yet anyway.

Lisa and I moved out of my parents' home and into the home of a wonderful couple from church who had two little girls. Greg and Katie were the youth pastors at Community Chapel and were two of the nicest people I had ever met.

Greg played keyboard on the worship team and used to tour with a pretty famous Christian band. I had never heard of the band, but I saw the gold albums on his wall so I knew it was true. Lisa and their girls played well together, so our living arrangement was a good fit.

Greg and Katie were very fond of Kris and me. Many nights I would talk with Katie about Kris. She reassured me that God would take care of him.

She also confirmed that Jessica was a she-devil, and she knew Kris was going to fall for her.

"Jessica has been the undoing of many men in our church," she said.

I was frightened for Kris. I still loved him but wasn't sure I should. It seemed like every waking hour I would pray to God about what to do.

"If this is not from You, God, and You have someone else for me, please take these feelings away."

The feelings, though, never subsided. I couldn't understand why I was being tortured. This was one of the most difficult times of my life. Going to church and seeing Jessica and Kris sitting together was too much for me to bear. I stopped going to the singles events because I couldn't handle seeing them together. I got an actual physical pain in the pit of my stomach every time I thought about Kris and Jessica.

I tried to move on. With all of my being I tried. Greg and Katie wanted to set me up with the drummer from Greg's former band. Even though I wasn't familiar with the band, I saw his pictures – long blond hair, blue eyes, and very handsome.

Without my knowing it, they invited him over one night to a group event they were hosting. He and I talked most of the night. I didn't know if he knew we were being set up, but if he did, he didn't seem to mind. At the end of the night, I walked him out to his car and we talked some more sitting on the curb.

"Well, I'm going to get going," he said. "It was really nice talking with you. You really don't know who I am, do you?"

"Sorry. I wasn't always around church people. I've never heard of you or your band."

Instead of being insulted, he found it refreshing.

"Would you like to go out next week?"

Before I could think of a response, I heard the answer leave my mouth.

"No, but it was sweet of you to ask."

"Can't blame a guy for trying. "We both smiled and I waved to him as he drove off.

Walking back to the house, I pondered what had just transpired. "No? What do you mean no? Cute, famous Christian rock star wants to take you out? What were you thinking?"

But I couldn't lead him on. If we were going to get together, I had to have Kris out of my head and out of my heart.

###

One night the Lord came to me and spoke again. I was to tell Kris that Jessica was evil and that he should be careful. I phoned him and gave him the warning. I also assured him that I was not trying to break them up. I was telling him because I cared about him and that was it.

As I hung up the phone, I honestly didn't know what God meant by being careful. I only felt I was required to deliver the message. A few weeks later I found out. My phone rang, and though I was guarded, it was a nice surprise to hear Kris's voice on the other end. He rarely phoned me at a late hour. We talked for a few minutes, then he said, "Would it be all right if I came over and hung out?" I knew something was up.

"Now?"

"Yeah, is that okay?"

"Sure, absolutely! See you in a bit."

Something had changed. He wasn't with Jessica anymore. He never said so, but I just knew.

At that time in my life, I began to doubt that I really had a "gift." I ignored a lot of what it told me, not understanding how I could know such things. I blew it off as craziness. I also didn't want to jump to conclusions. But the next Sunday Jessica and Kris were not sitting together in church.

Greg and Katie were to be the speakers at the young adult camping retreat, and Kris wanted to drive up with us. Because Jessica was going to the retreat, too, this confirmed they were no longer together.

I really felt I shouldn't have ill feelings toward Jessica. Even though she made me sick to my stomach, I knew that being bitter was not the answer. My intention was to talk to her that weekend. Don't talk about Kris, I told myself, simply be friendly.

All the girls at the retreat shared a very large room with bunk beds. Here I was stuck in the same room with Jessica.

She was pretty – a petite, skinny thing – and I was envious. I wasn't fat but always felt fatter than everyone else who was a size 5, maybe because of having big boobs. I never saw myself as pretty. Many of our friends said they couldn't believe Kris was with Jessica instead of me because I was so much prettier. That was very comforting, but I didn't see it.

I have to admit it was easier being around Jessica that weekend knowing she and Kris weren't together anymore. It was clear Kris had broken it off, but she still saw me as competition. I watched her try to sit next to him and appear as if they were still together, but I knew it wasn't true.

The last day of the retreat Kris and I were in the kitchen while everyone was packing up. I asked him directly if he and Jessica were still together, and he told me what I already knew.

"No, we are not together, and the warning you gave me to be careful turned out to be right on."

Kris didn't tell me why he broke up with Jessica, and I never asked. Months later he said he once saw her face change and take on the appearance of something demonic. It really scared him. Maybe God was showing him what he was really involved with.

###

As time passed, Kris and I began spending time together as before. One thing led to another, and soon we were drawn to each other sexually. I stopped using birth control. If a person wasn't supposed to have sex before marriage, there was no point in it. After only a few times with Kris, I became pregnant and knew it instantly.

I tried to tell Kris, but he didn't think I knew what I was talking about. He didn't understand or believe in my gift.

So, although I really knew I was pregnant, I waited to tell Kris until I had the results from the doctor. When it was official, I told Greg and Katie first. It was hard to tell them because Kris and I weren't supposed to be having sex and now everyone would know. I was so ashamed!

But from the moment I told them, they never judged us. At the time, Lisa and I shared a room in Greg and Katie's house. We agreed to put the three girls in the same room and have the baby stay with me. Katie and Greg made me feel a lot better. I wasn't expecting Kris to marry me, nor did I want him to out of obligation.

Greg and Katie gave me the courage to tell Kris. Kris was in shock. He knew he didn't want to make the same mistake he made with his son Steven, and wanted to be a part of this child's life. We told the pastor, who said we had to get married. Kris was a man of honor, so of course he would make things right. But I knew it was out of a sense of obligation and not deep love that he was talking marriage. He mentioned waiting until the baby was born and having his family come from Sweden for the wedding.

Kris was going on a men's retreat in a few weeks, and I figured that would give him the opportunity to sort things out. We were both still in shock at how quickly our circumstances were changing.

As my situation became the subject of gossip in the church, it became apparent that many people believed I became pregnant to trap Kris into marrying me. Nothing was further from the truth. When I learned I was pregnant, I didn't even expect him to marry me. So this rumor was very cruel and hurtful. On the other hand, many other church members surprised me with their kindness and understanding.

A week before the men's retreat, Greg came to us after church and said he felt the Lord said we should get married now and not wait.

"You mean before the baby's born?" I asked.

Greg was adamant about our getting married before Kris went on the men's retreat. We were both somewhat stunned, not sure what to make of this turn of events. As we left church and were driving to my parents' home, Kris turned to me and said, "So, you want to get married or what?"

Still numb from the meeting with Greg, I was in a daze. Did Kris just ask me to marry him? Was that really his proposal? He did say it with a smile, so how could I resist.

"Yes," I said.

It was actually kind of humorous because Kris used nearly the same words I spoke to him when I asked him out for the first time. "So, you want to go out or what?"

I had to plan my wedding within a week. And was still wondering whether this was really God's desire. That question was answered during the next few days.

Katie told me her friend from work made cakes, and she would have her make our wedding cake. People from the church said they would bring food for the reception. One of my colleagues at work got us a suite at a fancy hotel for our honeymoon. My parents arranged for the limousine.

The only thing left was my dress. Lisa's godmother Diane was about my size, so I asked if I could borrow her dress. She had much broader shoulders than I, and when I tried it on, it hung off my petite frame. She told me if it didn't change the dress too much, I could have it altered.

The owner of the dry cleaners near my house took one look at me in the dress and said it would take a lot of work to alter it. I stood in the dressing room with this beautiful wedding dress hanging off my shoulders and knew she was right.

Before I could think of another solution, God intervened. "What size are you, about a 5?" the woman asked.

"Yes," I answered, not knowing where she was heading.

"If you pay to have it dry cleaned, you can borrow my dress," she said.

In amazement, I agreed.

Five minutes later, I was in my car following her to her house. I couldn't believe what was happening. This woman was on a mission. A perfect stranger was lending me her wedding dress.

As we approached her home, I noticed the neighborhood was very upscale. We went high into the hills to Hacienda Heights, where she pulled into the driveway of a mansion and motioned me out of my car. Inside I followed her up the winding staircase and into her bedroom. She went straight to her closet and retrieved the dress.

"Ah. Here it is. Go try it on in there."

I gasped at the beauty of the elaborate dress. She ushered me into her changing room, which was as big as my bedroom. What happened next completed the gift from God. The dress fit perfectly.

I walked out of the dressing room, and the owner of this amazing dress beamed. She began positioning the eight-foot train and fussed over me as if I were her own daughter. She smoothed out every detail of the dress. Then she looked at me with a very contented expression. Her mission was complete.

"I knew it! I knew it would fit. Perfect, perfect. Come back to the dry cleaners in a few days, and it will be ready. Perfect, perfect."

This was surreal. Who does this for a total stranger? After I changed back into my clothes, she gave me a big hug and a kiss on both cheeks and walked me to the front door.

As I drove away, I realized I didn't even know her name.

A few days later, I went back to the dry cleaners to pick up the dress. It was there but the owner was not. I wanted to get her name and thank her for her extreme kindness. The person behind the counter quickly found the dress but didn't know the name of the owner, nor had she ever met her.

I did get to use Diane's veil, and her sister-in-law wore the same size shoe as I and let me use the shoes she wore in her wedding. That Wednesday I picked up everything and brought them home. When I put it all together, I couldn't believe my eyes. The beading on the shoes was exactly the same as that on the dress, and the veil was the same shade of white as the gown and shoes.

God did it! In one week we became Mr. and Mrs. Kris Nordahl.

CHAPTER 5

The Nightmare Begins

One difficult year had passed since that miraculous day, and now this. My flashbacks were coming on strong.

We were still attending Community Chapel, and Kris suggested I talk to the pastors about my disturbing visions and memories.

Unfortunately, the daughter pastor was no help, saying it sounded like I was going through healing from my past. She did not offer any support or help in how to work through the healing process. In truth, I didn't even know what I needed healing from. I came home from the meeting wondering why a person who ostensibly was a servant of God could leave me hanging like that. I had many questions and not many answers.

As I grew in my faith, my lifestyle changed.

Hidden!

Something I noticed in the past year was that not everyone who claimed to believe in God seemed committed to Him. Simply going to church didn't make someone a person of character or integrity. Kris would tease me for being so gullible and believing that all people who went to church made a difference in the world.

I also noticed people leaving the church. The pastor would say to us on Sunday morning, "If you see anyone outside of church who no longer attends our church, do not speak to them. They have backslidden and have fallen away from God."

I was stunned. Why would anyone want to leave God?

At the grocery store one day, I saw someone who had left the church. Her name was Teresa, and she was a friend of mine, though I hadn't heard from her in a long time. What was I to do? The pastor said not to talk to people who had left the church.

Teresa came right up to me. "Hey, long time, no see."

I couldn't just ignore her, so I said, "Hey, yes, it has been a long time. How come we haven't seen you?"

"My family and I are going to the Four Square Church around the corner," she said. "We really like it."

"Really?"

Wow! This struck me as unbelievable, yet I was exhilarated. Teresa and her family hadn't fallen away from God at all. They just changed churches.

I was so excited when I got home that I shared the great news with Kris. Then I noticed him grinning.

"What? What's so funny?"

"You really believed that they were backslidden if they left the church?"

I didn't know what to say. Why would the pastors lie? Why shouldn't I have believed them? That was my first wakeup call. Christians were no different from non-Christians except they accepted Christ as their Savior and the others didn't.

My flashes of evil were worse than ever. They would come at random times of the day and without warning. There was no controlling it. I could be at work or cooking dinner. I was short with the girls, now 3 and

8, and didn't pay much attention to the husband I loved.

Kris was becoming impatient with me. We seemed to argue about insignificant things more frequently. He finally told me either I had to get help or he would leave.

What I didn't realize was that each frame of my flashes was a story unfolding from my past – a story that had been buried deep within my subconscious.

One night while I was sleeping, all the frames of those many flashes came together. This was no dream. It was a horrendous vision from my past flooding my conscious mind.

The dark presence I had experienced was my oldest brother. I saw a familiar girl crying on the floor of a room while he was touching her in ways a little girl should never be touched.

I woke up sweating and breathing heavily, wondering if my dream was real. It all came rushing in. A door had been unlocked.

How could I have forgotten such a horrific act? How could something be pushed so deep into the subconscious that it was as if it had never happened?

This was bigger than anything I had ever dealt with. Why had I not remembered seeing this? Suppressing what I saw must be at the root of my unusual behavior. I needed to find someone who was familiar with these types of situations.

Lately we had been visiting another church on Sunday evenings and I found out it had a support program for people in my situation. I made an appointment to see the counselors. Many questions raced through my mind. Where did this happen? Why was I there? How did my brother get away with it? Did I do anything to help this little girl? So many questions.

My first appointment was with two incredible ladies who had the gift of making people feel at ease while they talked through whatever needed discussing. They helped me with all I had suppressed and was now remembering oh so well. Now that the gates to the memories were unlocked, more and more came rushing in.

During my first appointment with the people who would be my counselors for the next four weeks, I had to explain everything I saw. As I spoke, the process of telling about it led to more and more of the situation being revealed. I realized that the abuse of this little girl had been happening from the time she was about eight years old until she was in fifth grade, a span of two to three years.

The week after that first visit was a blur. The whole period from my childhood that I had blocked out was becoming more real to me than the present day.

During my second visit, a tiny object was placed on the floor across the room from me. I was told to pretend that the object was my brother and to tell him how I felt about what he had done to that little girl. This was not easy. As I began to speak, fear gripped me as if my brother were a threat to me. Perhaps he found out that I knew his secret and threatened me at some point in my young life. I wasn't sure. I only knew the fear was daunting. The only thing I could come up with to say was, "Why? Why would you do this – steal a little girl's innocence? Cause her to be afraid in her own home, in her own room? How could you rob her of the security and safety of her home?"

In between visits to the counselors, more and more memories returned, which gave way to more questions. How did I know this happened in the girl's home and in her room, and why was I there to witness such a horrific act?

On the third visit, I had to write a letter to my brother. The counselors assured me that it would not be mailed until I was ready for it to be. Again, fear gripped me at the thought of this letter accidentally being mailed.

After the fourth and last visit, I was advised to join a support group at the church. It would run for nine weeks, and for the two weeks before it began, I was to come back and receive something called "soaking prayer." Four or five people who were trained in praying for others would spend an hour each time praying for me. This would be a time of preparation to receive healing and have an open heart for what the Lord was going to do through the support group.

I didn't understand how a person could be trained to pray for someone. But I did know my counselors. They knew what they were doing and were the first people to actually help me. I took their advice and did as they suggested.

The prayer time was spent with many tears. Again, I wasn't sure what was happening. All I knew was the atmosphere was very peaceful. These precious people would pray for me, and I would weep profusely. At the end of each session, I would feel as if someone cleaned me on the inside. I felt cleansed and refreshed.

###

On my drive home after the second "soaking prayer" session, I decided I had to ask my friend Diane, who was Lisa's godmother and had offered to lend me her wedding dress a few years earlier, to come with me to the support group meetings. What I didn't know was that my gift was at work once again. The thought never entered my mind that she might need the support group herself. I was just terrified and didn't want to go alone.

But when I explained to Diane what I had been through -- the flashbacks, the dark memories, the last four weeks of counseling, prayer, and now this support group -- the first thing out of her mouth was, "How did you know?"

I didn't answer her because at the time I didn't know anything, at least I didn't think I did. She gladly accepted my invitation.

So it began. Every Monday Diane would come straight from work to my home to pick me up. I would make her a plate of dinner, and she would eat while I drove the thirty minutes to the group.

The first night, much to our surprise, there were two support groups, and Diane and I were split up. We were each given a book to read and a workbook in which to do homework. As Diane and I drove home after each meeting, we would talk about what we went through in our separate groups. It turned out that she had been molested when she was little. That was really all she had to tell me, and I knew the rest.

For example, I knew her dad was the culprit. These group meetings were helping us, and as we shared with each other, more and more unfolded.

Unfortunately, I wasn't just dealing with old memories. I also had to raise a family and have a relationship with Kris. As time went on, I didn't feel comfortable when Kris touched me, and this did not sit well with him. As if our relationship wasn't strained enough, now this.

I couldn't explain it to him. All I knew was that I felt dirty and uncomfortable whenever he touched me. I would share with him, hoping he would understand all that had unfolded. Every exercise the counselors did with me, the prayer sessions, everything from the group sessions that wasn't confidential, I shared it all. He wanted to understand, but there was no way he could comprehend what Diane and I were experiencing.

As I worked through the workbook, it was as if the author had been inside my brain and wrote all that I felt on those pages.

One night while doing my homework, I had another memory of the little girl and my step brother. Only this time I saw the girl more clearly than ever before, and then it hit me: To my horror, I was not merely in that room witnessing these shocking acts, I *was* the little girl.

How had I missed that? The next thing I knew, my mind was reeling, remembering years of abuse by my brother.

Then a memory of a later time of my life tore through my mind, and it was far worse than remembering my brother coming into my room each night.

My family moved from Colorado to California when I was about fifteen, and I became extremely homesick for my friends and the place where I grew up. The rest of my family, my aunts, uncles, and cousins, were in Colorado, so my parents didn't see any harm in my going back for a visit.

My aunt let me stay a night with my girlfriend, whom I had known practically all my life. She and I went to the mountains with a group of people I didn't know. Everyone was drinking alcohol and smoking pot. I even think some were taking acid. I had never really drunk alcohol before, but this was an older crowd and I didn't want them to think I was too young to be part of their group, so I joined in.

After that first drink, the rest became spotty. We all drove back to someone's house. I had had too much to drink and was passed out. A guy I vaguely remembered talking with earlier in the night carried me up to a bedroom. I was semi-conscious but had no functionality of my body parts. It was as if I was having an out-of-body experience. I knew what was happening, but I couldn't speak or move.

Soon the guy was taking off my pants, and I knew I did not like where this was going and what he was about to do. Even though I was still a virgin, I wasn't ignorant about what was happening to me. As I lay there helpless, the door opened. I saw a silhouette in the doorway and thought to myself, "I'm rescued!"

I tried to yell, but only a whispered "Help" came out. A girl who had not known we were in the room and thought she was intruding immediately shut the door.

When the guy had done his deed, he got up and left.

As my mind returned to the present day, I sat in my bedroom grappling with this memory. I had just witnessed how I lost my virginity. How could I have not remembered that?

I learned later that a person goes into survival mode and suppresses certain experiences that can't be dealt with. But I no longer needed to be in survival mode. In order to heal, all that was buried had to be dug up. I couldn't deal with it if I couldn't remember it.

However, I still felt like a frightened little girl. When I opened the workbook that first week, I no longer had the same view of life.

PART II

CHAPTER 6

Warning Signs

Something startled me awake, and my body jerked. I sat up. I must have fallen asleep doing my homework.

It must still be daylight because it's extremely bright in here.

Yet something was wrong. I adjusted my eyes to the brightness and looked around.

Where am I?

This was not my room, although it was a beautiful white room with a queen-size bed covered by a delicate pale pink duvet. Against the wall was a feminine little dressing table with a lighted mirror.

I noticed an open arch-shaped window with no glass or screen. The sheer curtain that covered it was billowing slightly from the light breeze.

That's strange. I am always cold and yet the breeze feels warm and pleasant. The temperature is perfect.

I scooted off the bed and saw that I had my own bathroom and my own fireplace. Sweet!

Wait a minute, Michelle. Why aren't you freaked out? Maybe I hadn't woken up after all and this was a dream. I slowly inched my way to the bathroom, turned on the cold water and splashed my face.

If I'm asleep, this will wake me up….maybe I am awake. I'm pretty wet to still be sleeping. This is not a dream!

I walked out of the bathroom to try to see exactly what this place was. The entryway to my room also was arched, and the door fit perfectly in the arch. It reminded me of a door in a castle. Vertical wood beams with two black metal pieces lay horizontally, one at the top of the door and one at the bottom. I peeked out the door down the long, wide hallway. Nothing was dark about this place; everything was white. Even the wood floor was whitewashed.

I ventured down the hall past many other arch-shaped entries toward a long, winding staircase. The staircase was like something I had seen in old movies from the 1950s. I looked back down the hall wondering about those rooms. What or who was in them?

But the rooms would have to wait as I was even more curious about the rest of the place.

I tiptoed my way to the staircase and looked down at the open area below. Apparently there were no children running around here since nearly everything was white. Either that or they had a meticulous cleaning crew. In fact, the only color I saw was the pale pink duvet in my room.

I crept down the stairs ever so carefully. Not knowing where I was, I didn't want someone to discover me before I discovered them. At the bottom of the stairs was a large, open room with a crescent-shaped couch in front of another fireplace.

As I looked around I observed more arch-shaped windows that were also wide open.

Along with no children, there must be no insects here.

The double front doors, of course, were also arch-shaped and of the same design as the doors upstairs. The ceiling was vaulted.

My stomach was growling, and as I continued investigating, I wondered if there was a kitchen and food. I next came to a great dining room with a tiered chandelier and a dining table for twelve.

Hidden!

Perhaps I'm not here alone. If not, is that good or bad?

I continued my journey to find food. The dining room traditionally is next to the kitchen, and behold, not only a kitchen, but a spacious one. Still not knowing where I was or why I was here, I opened the refrigerator with hopes of finding something to eat. Much to my delight there was everything imaginable.

My hunger pains got the best of me and I made a sandwich.

With this fully stocked kitchen, it's likely someone else is here.

Noticing a back door from the kitchen, I took my sandwich and walked outside. Maybe I could recognize something that would give me a clue where I was.

What a contrast the outside was from the white inside. So much color. The perfectly cut grass was a deep green such as I had never before seen. I had to touch it. It didn't feel like any grass I was familiar with but rather like cotton. Colorful flowers graced the grounds and a turquoise waterfall cascaded through rocks to a pond surrounded by more rocks. There was no fence.

I walked around the building, which from the outside reminded me of a medieval castle – except that it was as white on the outside as on the inside.

Over the double-door entry were the words Vic'tim Mentala.

This must be some type of a hotel or bed and breakfast. I looked at the word again and said it out loud. The t-i-m I pronounced like team. "Vic'team Mentala."

Huh! Interesting, I wonder what it means.

As stunning as the grounds were, I was drawn back inside.

This time I walked through the front door, and much to my surprise, there were people there. Now I knew this had to be a hotel of some sort.

Did Kris give me a sleeping pill and fly me off to France or Italy for a romantic vacation?

That would be a dream. We didn't have the money, and if we did, Kris wouldn't spend it on that. He would use the money to make more money. Besides, Kris was not the romantic type.

I have often wondered if in the back of his mind he thought I trapped him into marrying me. He seemed so distant, as if he were only in the marriage to be obedient to God.

Then a familiar face invaded my thoughts. It was Jamie from my support group. Weird! Coming into focus were other familiar faces. Ten to be exact; some seemed to be from my support group. Where did they come from? The bigger question was where were we?

I called and motioned her over. "Jamie." She came running over like a giddy little child. "Isn't this place great?" she asked.

Her voice was carefree, but I answered in a reluctant tone,

"I guess it would be if I knew where here is."

Just as I said that, a peaceful feeling of familiarity came over me. At that moment, a booming voice emanated from the top of the stairs. The speaker was a large man, probably in his seventies, with white hair, tanned skin and wearing loose-fitting linen pants and a tunic top. His outfit reminded me of what men in the Middle East wear. He had a serene presence and almost floated down the stairs. I asked Jamie who he was, and she looked at me and giggled. "He's the one who invited us here, silly."

Okay, I thought, we're on a retreat. I must have been knocked out on the bus ride here because I did not remember any of this. I walked over to another girl, Kim, who wasn't quite as excited to be here as Jamie.

"How long is this retreat again?"

She looked at me, squinting her eyes suspiciously, and said, "We can stay as long as we like."

As long as we like? I wasn't sure I had decided to be here in the first place.

Something else was nagging at me. Where was Diane? How could she have missed this?

The elderly man was now at the bottom of the stairs and invited us to sit at the dining table with the twelve chairs.

As we drew near, he stood at the head of the table and introduced himself as Mr. Kripling. He had a nice voice, his tone almost like a song.

I had no recollection of ever meeting Mr. Kripling, but it was one of those times when you meet a person and feel as though you have known him all your life. He explained that we would have a chance to sit in a different chair each time we sat at the table.

This didn't make sense to me at first, as I walked around the table. But as I looked more closely, I noticed words written on the back of each one: GETTING STARTED, WARNING SIGNS, FACING THE BATTLE, STAGES OF ABUSE, SHAME, CONTEMPT, POWERLESSNESS, AMBIVALENCE, BETRAYAL, MANNERISM, REPENTANCE, and BOLD LOVE.

This was definitely a retreat, and I was actually feeling a hint of excitement about what the days ahead might hold. We all came around the table, and I found myself in front of the chair that read "GETTING STARTED."

I am a very structured person – everything should have an order – and I always play by the rules. It was fate that I stood at this chair. How could one start anywhere else? We all took our seats, and in front of us on the table were our workbooks. I didn't remember packing, much less bringing my workbook. Mr. Kripling instructed us to open our workbooks and share what we had written. I didn't recall having written anything. He looked at me. "GETTING STARTED will begin."

Opening my book, I thought to myself, how am I supposed to share when I haven't even written anything? Reluctantly, I opened my book and, not only was there handwriting on the pages, it was mine. I didn't remember writing anything, but then why should that surprise me considering the way this day had gone so far. My heart pounded as I read the words from my book aloud.

"Where Am I Today?" was the heading. "I'm feeling hopeful, angry, fearful. I feel like an outcast. I am likely to hurt others with my anger.

"When I'm dealing with an issue, it becomes very strenuous. I tend to get irritated by the smallest things and snap, usually at those around me. Ultimately this adds to stress, and I feel guilty and foolish for letting things get to me.

"I am emotionally handicapped and somehow less of a person because of it. I feel as if something is wrong with me, like I have a hidden disease. It's very difficult to talk to people because I don't appear normal, and they are. I fear God is not going to protect me. He didn't before, so why would he now?

"Although I am encouraged that one day I may actually feel stable and be able to deal with my emotions, I am discouraged that there may be issues I cannot face. What scares me is: What if being in this support group doesn't work?

"I desperately want to be rid of my anger, but sometimes I feel I am doomed to live with it. I'm hoping for a release, a clearer view of what's going on inside of me and how to deal with it. I'm also afraid to hope for genuine joy because I know it won't last. Good feelings are always invaded by bad ones."

My turn was over, and each of the others shared where they were today. They didn't always address what the sign on their chair said like we were supposed to. They weren't following the rules and that bothered me.

By now it was late and we all retreated upstairs to our rooms. At the top of the stairs, I looked down the hallway to all the rooms I had seen earlier. Obviously this is where the others were staying, so I was no longer curious about them.

When I returned to the room I assumed was mine, my body was weary and my mind confused by all that happened during the day. A pair of white pajamas lay on my bed. I slipped into them and into bed.

Was it my imagination or was my duvet a bit darker shade of pink than it was before? As I leaned over to turn off the lamp, I saw a card on the night stand. It read, "To be continued…" How kind. A welcome card. I wondered if everyone received a card saying the same thing. I also wondered if, when I woke up, I would still be here or at home. I supposed, though, that the card had answered that question.

The next morning I was still at Vic'tim Mentala. For a moment, I secretly felt like a princess trapped in a castle, waiting for a knight in shining armor. I imagined Kris on his white horse coming to my rescue. I always wanted Kris to be my hero, but it didn't seem like he wanted the role.

I slid out of bed and exchanged my white pajamas for a white linen dress that was left on the chair. Perhaps everything was still all white, but it sure appeared that the curtains had become the same pale pink as the duvet.

Heading downstairs, I was curious about what today would bring. I must have slept the longest because it seemed everyone else was present and accounted for. Even Mr. Kripling was mingling among the other ten. I rounded the corner into the dining room and beheld a beautiful table set with assorted fruit – mangoes, grapes, various melons – along with scrambled eggs and toast, all my favorite breakfast foods.

I felt a hand on my shoulder and looking behind me saw Mr. Kripling.

"Well, hello, Sunshine, sleep well?"

"I, I did, yes, thank you."

He was so familiar to me. Where did I know him from? He gathered the others around the table, and I caught a glimpse of my chair, MANNERISM. As everyone began eating breakfast, I prayed silently to myself, not wanting to draw attention, then began to eat.

Mr. Kripling announced the task at hand. "You will spend a day with each personality here."

Oh, I get it. He wanted us all to get to know each other better. I wasn't comfortable with that. I like people as a rule, but before long everyone will know everyone else's business and then the gossip will begin. It's pointless.

After we finished eating, Mr. Kripling announced, "No need to clean up; it will be taken care of. Please proceed to your assignment."

I made a beeline for the back door, really wanting to get outside and away from everyone. I opened the back door and there to my horror stood one of the ten.

"Hello, I'm Mary. We're supposed to meet." A reluctant hello was my response as she stepped inside and walked toward a room I hadn't noticed earlier. I followed, partially because I didn't want to be rude and partially because getting to know everyone was probably inevitable anyway. Also I was curious about the room. It had a large desk with a chair behind it and a chaise lounge stationed in front. French doors opened onto a patio. Mary sat behind the desk and motioned me to sit on the chaise lounge. It was a bit awkward, but I went along with it.

"Where are you from, Mary?"

"Where are you from, Michelle?"

How did she know my name? She had introduced herself, but I never said who I was.

"How do you know my name?"

"Everyone knows you."

Everyone knows me? Is that what she said? Suddenly I had many questions.

"Why does everyone know me?"

"You're the reason we're all here."

Now I was really confused.

"What exactly do you mean?"

"It's simple. You are why we came. You need to loosen up and go with the flow. Just behave the way we all expect you to, and you will get along fine."

I really wasn't sure I wanted to get along "fine." Besides how was I supposed to know how to behave?

"What else do I need to know?"

"Well, don't go hanging around outside too much, or they will all think you're weird. We only talk about certain things, nothing too personal. We all have been hurt and have developed our own set of strategies to keep from getting hurt again, so don't interfere with that process. It's also acceptable to doubt whether we can trust God, since He's done a pathetic job of protecting us so far. We need to focus on how to protect ourselves from never being taken advantage of again."

Wow! This lady is nuts.

"Is there anything else?" I began to feel anger come over me, but I wasn't sure why.

"Yes, there's a lot more, but this will help you survive for now."

I wanted to ask more questions or maybe even have a conversation, but I wasn't sure how that would go over. I was very conscious of what the rules were and didn't want her to think of me as being weird or out of the ordinary.

After being in Mary's presence awhile, I became aware of how much I cared about what she thought of me. It was as if she dictated who I was, and if I didn't meet her expectations, then somehow I was less of a person. I began to feel that way about everyone there that day. I wondered what they must think of me. How should I act in order to be accepted? Well, Mary gave me the rules, so if I followed them, I should be seen as normal.

As I looked through the French doors, something outside tugged at me, almost beckoning me to come and join it. Then I remembered Mary's words, "Don't hang outside too much or else they will think you're weird."

At that moment Mary opened the desk drawer and pulled out a book, opened it and began reading silently. I waited a bit, thinking she was going to share some more. Or perhaps she was reading something important and would share that with me. So I sat and waited. After what seemed to be an hour, I didn't know what to do.

"Is that a good book?" I asked finally.

"Mmmm-Hmmm."

Gosh, do I continue to sit here? Do I get up and leave? Can I leave? What do I do? I sat a bit longer and looked through the French doors some more. It was as if I could hear the wind calling me.

I've never been the outdoorsy type, so what was it that was summoning me ever so strongly? Again, the rules came back to me about not spending too much time out there. Oh well, it was a nice thought.

Then something interrupted my daydreaming. Mary was walking toward the door of the room. I looked over at the desk and saw that the book lay face down. My curiosity got the better of me, and, confirming that Mary was gone, I scrambled over to it. The title read "*WHO YOU CHOOSE TO BE*." *Must be one of those self-help books.*

I opened the book, and the pages were blank.

Really. Mary had sat there for two hours looking at blank pages and made me sit there waiting for her. I looked up as the outdoors called again. I was angry that Mary made me sit there doing nothing, wondering what the heck was going on. I walked over and opened the French doors. As my feet hit the patio, I felt the cold on the bottoms of my feet and remembered I didn't have on any shoes. I was not accustomed to wearing shoes indoors at my home, or in anyone else's home.

I took in the beauty of the outdoors. There was a lake so still it looked like blue glass. Tall trees lined the lake, and beyond the trees were rolling hills of greens and blue-greens. It was as if the trees were dancing upon the hills. I'd heard of blue grass so maybe this was it. Beyond the hills a blue sky provided a beautiful backdrop.

I was so caught up in the splendor of that moment I didn't realize the time. The sun was dipping below the hills. It was getting dark. But I took one more look. Turning to walk back inside I caught a fleeting glimpse of the cement benches on the patio. Something was on one of them. It stood out because the cement benches were, of course, white and this thing was not.

What was it? I already spent too much time out here, but I had to know. Quickly I ran over to the bench. It was a rose made of red granite. Strangely beautiful. Strangely mesmerizing. It held my gaze for a few moments, and when I came to myself, I snatched it up and rushed back inside. I carefully closed the doors so no one would know that I wandered outside.

Since it was getting dark, dinner was probably being served, and it would once again be time to share. Rushing past the desk, I was compelled to run back and grab the book. With the granite rose and blank-paged book, I scurried out of the room, careful not to be seen. I don't know why I felt like I was doing something wrong but I had to hide what was in my hands. I dashed up the stairs straight for my room, hid my treasures under my bed, and ran back down the stairs.

I slowed my pace as I approached the dinner table. I still didn't know why I felt the need to hide my items. It just seemed likely they would be taken away if someone found them. And I knew somehow that I needed them in order to survive this place.

Everyone was chatting and it looked as if no one even noticed my absence. Mr. Kripling wasn't around either, so I must not have been late. One of the servants entered the room and announced that Mr. Kripling would not be joining us for dinner but would come later for the time of sharing.

Everyone took their seats and began to eat. Again I said a silent blessing so no one would notice. I saw that the servants all wore white, which made sense because that was probably their uniform. The clothing of the others around me was varied. Some wore white like me; some all beige. Others had glimmers of color in their wardrobes.

Scanning the crowd, I spotted Mary. She was being very quiet. She saw me and shot me a glaring glance before looking back at her food and eating. What was with the look she gave me? I wondered.

Then with horror, I thought to myself, she knows. She knows I took her book. She probably went back to retrieve it and found it gone. Who else would have taken it except me? I was the only one there. I wondered how I was going to get out of this one.

Mr. Kripling's soothing voice interrupted my panicky thoughts and I was immediately set at ease as he asked us to bring our chairs into the den and sit around the fireplace for our share time.

My chair tonight read WARNING SIGNS. Oh good, someone else would go first tonight, I thought. I had way too much on my mind as I kept an eye on Mary, waiting for her to say something about the book.

As we took our seats in the den, my thoughts began to wander. Why were we sharing? What's the point?

So many questions but no one to answer them. Everyone else seemed to know what was going on, and I didn't want anyone to think I was odd and in the dark.

All my life, I would hide that I didn't know certain things I thought were obvious to others so they wouldn't think I was stupid.

Then Mr. Kripling looked at me and said something that made absolutely no sense. "WARNING SIGNS, you will go first."

Hidden!

"But Getting Started should go first," I said.

There it was, that fear of what they must think. Did I just break the rules? Did I speak out of turn? Not good, not good. The silence from everyone made it worse.

Then I realized the silence was my cue to pretend I never said that and to proceed. The book I had the night before now lay on the coffee table in front of me. Again, with no recollection of writing anything, I was surprised to see words on the page in my very own handwriting.

"I used to feel that this *thing* couldn't possibly be the main reason for my anger, impatience, control issues, and personality faults," I began. "I always thought I was cursed and I could never change no matter how hard I tried to control my temper. I never realized how many aspects of my personality were linked to my sexual abuse. I didn't realize how vast the experience was.

"I also didn't make the connection to how my parents' lack of involvement in my life affected my attitude toward them. The way they dealt with matters in silence dictated my lack of self worth. This also distorted my view of how God saw me. I have always genuinely thought I was a bad person, and no matter how much I wanted to be a good person I was incapable of making that happen.

"It wasn't that I doubted something devastating happened to me. It's just that I didn't realize the impact it would have on my entire life. When I am stressed, I am short and impatient with people and not as kind and polite as I would normally be – especially when things don't go according to my plans. Sometimes I also get quiet and don't want to interact or participate in anything until I get a grip on my anger."

No one commented on what I read. Then the others began to share. I didn't even listen as thoughts of the day ran through my mind. My gaze went toward the window again and the puzzling contrast of all the color outside versus the stark whiteness inside. Even the dark night showed colors, which made the contrast from inside even richer.

When the sharing came to an end, we went back to our rooms with no issues having been addressed. No one said anything about what each of us shared. When I got to my room, I remembered my treasures under the bed, and somehow the thought of them comforted me. I turned on the lamp and reached for them. Lying on my bed, I looked at the rose, so beautiful and so intricate. The leaves, the shape of the petals, the smoothness of the granite. Where did it come from?

For some reason, it reminded me of Kris. He gave me flowers only one time that I can recall, and yet the rose almost spoke his name.

Next I turned my attention to the book with blank pages. This didn't make any sense. I recalled the scene in the den. Mary was sitting at the desk pretending to read the blank pages. That was rude. Thinking about her truly made me angry. Even so, I cared about what she thought of me. Why?

I closed the book and read the title on the cover. It read, "WHO YOU CHOOSE TO BE." Huh! I read it again and again. "WHO YOU CHOOSE TO BE." "WHO YOU CHOOSE TO BE." "WHO YOU CHOOSE TO BE."

I fell asleep repeating those words and imagined what I would be like if I could actually choose who I could be. When I was little, I never wanted to be in my family. I wished I could be in my friend's family, who seemed to have everything. They had a big house and nice cars. She wore all the latest fashions. Even when I liked a boy, she got him and I didn't.

###

The light coming in my window woke me up. Seeing the rose and book brought back the events of the previous day. I looked at the granite rose and the card still on my night stand, and for some reason I was compelled to hug them. I really missed Kris and wondered how my girls were doing. My girls are my life, and I couldn't imagine how everyone was managing without my being there to tell them what to do.

I also remembered the words on the cover of the book and read them once again: *"WHO YOU CHOOSE TO BE."* I opened the book to the first page, and lo and behold there were words there. They were typed, as if the book were being written before me. It read, "Today is the first day of the rest of your life."

Wow, if only that were true. I again hugged my treasures and put them in the drawer of my night stand and got up to greet the day. I straightened the duvet and noticed it was definitely a brighter pink this morning. And my curtains were becoming the same shade of pink. I had slept in my clothes, and it seemed my dress was now a very pale pink as well.

My first thought was that it was probably the reflection from my duvet. But it was nice to see me in pale pink against so much bland white. I like white but only in small doses. I was discovering that color was so much more exciting now that my life was largely devoid of it.

As I began to get cleaned up, I noticed there was also a lightness about me. I thought about Mary and how rude she had been, pretending to read that book. Much to my amazement, I discovered I was no longer angry with her, though I imagined the anger would return once I saw her.

Then the words "*WHO YOU CHOOSE TO BE*" rang out in my heart. I remembered the book. Books represent knowledge, and I became distinctly aware that whether to be angry at Mary was a choice I could make. I didn't have to be angry. I could choose not to be. Now there was something I had never thought of. Wow! I felt a sensation of surrender come over me.

Next my attention turned to the rose. That lovely granite rose somehow gave me strength not to focus so much on what others might think of me but on whom I could be. This, however, would take more boldness than I thought I had.

I suddenly became aware that I granted others the power to dictate who I was. My choices have been based on what I assumed others were thinking of me. Why do I concern myself with what individuals might believe of me? The story I'm making up regarding what others are thinking of me may not even be true.

Then it hit me. I was giving people I don't even know the power to dictate who I am. I continued my ritual of washing my face and brushing my teeth as I processed these thoughts. Leaving on the dress I had slept in, I liked the idea that it might be a slight shade of pink and not white, even if that was just a reflection of the duvet. Being a bit different was somehow not so scary. It was even a bit adventurous. What was this peculiar new sensation brewing inside of me?

CHAPTER 7

In Control

Taking the journey downstairs, I had a new mindset toward whether I was going to let anyone dictate who I am. Although, I didn't even know who that truly was. I also wondered who I was going to meet today.

As I entered the foyer at the bottom of the stairs, immediately I sensed a different vibe about the place. Many people were in a hurry, rushing around the place. Why did I always get left out? No matter what the time of day, this place is always full of activity.

This morning was different though. Everyone was in a hurry, but to do what? And another thing, where were those people with the glimmer of color in their clothes. Today everyone was wearing pure white. Perhaps some of the people who were here yesterday had changed into white clothing. But, no. as I scanned the room, the others with colored clothing were nowhere to be found.

I did not recognize many of those bustling around the castle. They must be new here, possibly trying to make a good impression on Mr. Kripling.

Finally I saw a familiar face and called out to Jamie, who I saw the first day I was here.

"What's all the rush?"

"Breakfast time you know," she squealed with her cheery disposition.

"Are we late? Where is Mr. Kripling?"

"Gone for the day."

She then explained that after breakfast we were still to meet someone new. Still not sure why everything was so chaotic, I went into the kitchen and could not believe my eyes. Food was everywhere, and not all of it was breakfast food. Some people were eating sandwiches, others leftovers from dinner, and still others sweets.

This was extremely disturbing. They were all out of control! What should I do? Anything?

When I'm confused, I become very unsure of myself and tend not to follow what my gift is telling me to do. I then begin to doubt myself and do nothing at all. Confusion causes me to freeze.

Here I go again caring what others might think if I stepped out of my comfort zone and put things in proper order.

Then I decided to get a bowl of cereal. It was simple and hardly anyone would notice. Casually, I got a bowl and grabbed whatever cereal there was even if it wasn't my favorite. I would be noticed more if I started looking through the different kinds of cereal to get the one I really wanted. And I wasn't willing to risk how that might look. Finding the milk, I sat there among the noisy chaos and ate my breakfast.

Something told me this was not going to be a good day – another dreaded day of meeting someone new. Why am I here? I don't even like this place. It was interesting at first, but now it's gotten a little creepy.

A voice invaded my thoughts: "Why do you prejudge the outcome of the day before you even know what it holds?"

Startled not only by the voice but by the words, I turned to see a young man talking to me. First, how did he know what I was thinking, and, second, how dare he tell me that I prejudge situations? He continued to talk, apparently assuming I wanted to hear what he had to say.

"What experiences or people have you lost in your life by prejudging the outcome of something?

"Do you know why you fail at what's important to you?"

I was completely caught off guard. "No, I don't."

"You're so concerned about coming across as a phony that in the end you become one. You sacrifice what you truly want to do, be, or believe for the sake of looking good. In the process, you lose out on everything, including looking good."

"First of all," I replied, very annoyed, "who are you to be telling me anything about myself? You don't even know me."

He looked at me with a smirk, and with a sarcastic tone, replied, "Oh that's rich. What are you committed to? Do you have the courage to be real, to be the person you are instead of the one you think you should be? Ya know, it's more than acceptable to be you."

Once again, I was speechless. I had to think about what he said and why he said it.

"What's your name?"

"David. I guess you're my new partner today."

Not wanting to be rude, I said, "I guess so."

"It's pretty crazy around here, huh?"

"Yes, this is ridiculous, not at all what I had in mind."

"Oh? What did you have in mind?"

I explained that if it were done correctly, someone would be cooking while others set the table. Then we would all eat together and clean up together. From there we would choose our partners for the day and proceed with our assignment.

"But this way, nothing's going to get done right. Look, no one is even attempting to get a partner. They are all sitting around talking with anyone and everyone. If Mr. Kripling were here, this would not be happening."

"So you like being in control."

That was a strange question – or was it a statement?

"Of course, who doesn't?" It was so strange to be thought of as a control freak. I never looked at myself that way.

"What happens when you're not in control of a situation?"

"Well, I am very leery of my surroundings and try to gain control of them."

"Do you trust God?"

I'm usually the one with all the questions, and this was unfamiliar territory. It was becoming difficult to think of answers. I felt like my thought processes were somehow blocked.

"Of course, I trust God."

"So who's in control of your life, you or Him?"

"Well, of course, He is, right?"

"You tell me, Michelle, how does it go over with you when a situation doesn't go according to your plans?"

There he goes again. I don't remember telling him my name. Who is this person? I know his name is David, but who is he really? What did he mean by, "Oh that's rich" when I told him he didn't know me.

"Well, I don't like it when things don't go my way." There, I said it.

"What are you afraid of?"

Who said I was afraid of anything? As if he had read my thoughts once again, he continued.

"What if something doesn't go your way or you might not be in control of a situation? Or the outcome isn't exactly as you thought it should be? What are you afraid of?"

"It's my turn to ask the questions; you've already said plenty."

###

With that, a familiar voice rang out. It was Mr. Kripling at last. What a relief. Now he'll see this mess and that no one else is doing their assignments. Little did I realize that David and I had talked for the better part of the day.

I looked around and the kitchen was completely clean. But there were still those in groups who hadn't selected partners like we had been instructed to do. I eagerly waited to hear them get in trouble for being in groups.

But instead Mr. Kripling's wonderful voice rang out,

"It's once again share time."

Excuse me?

"Since it's still early, this evening we will share first and then have dinner. It looks like everyone has had a productive day."

A productive day? Is he kidding me? If he had seen this place earlier, he would not be saying that. Does he not see people in groups, people without partners? I don't feel very productive. I didn't even get a chance to talk with David about why he's here.

Then I realized I didn't even know what I wanted to ask David. Something about him was so familiar. Before we joined the others, he smiled and said one last thing. "You know, you can have more than one partner. You simply had a pre-conceived idea of what today was supposed to look like, and when it didn't match your assumptions, you placed it into the category of 'wrong.' So back to my original question, what did you miss out on by prejudging the outcome of today's situation?"

Clearly that was a rhetorical question, and David didn't expect an answer. He got off his stool and proceeded to the dining table. I understood what he asked and why he asked it, but I didn't have an answer. I was going to have to ponder the conversation with David, specifically his departing question.

Do I prejudge the outcome of events? Do I project my own thought processes on others without taking the time to discover what they actually intend?

I suppose I do, and perhaps that's why everything has to be a certain way. "When it didn't match your assumptions, you placed it into the category of 'wrong.'" He had said "WRONG" like it were a disease. But there are right and wrong ways of doing things, aren't there?

Absorbed in my thoughts, I looked around the room, and it was as if I had gone back in time to that morning. The chaos was back. Everyone was eating whatever they wanted for breakfast. People were talking in groups instead of choosing partners, and no one noticed I was there. Had I really gone back in time? I tested it out by walking around the room to hear the conversations.

I came to the first group. Those who were eating sandwiches had been up since dawn and already had breakfast.

The next group of "violators" was those eating leftovers. I heard them express how much they enjoyed dinner the night before and couldn't wait to see if there was anything left. They, too, had been up for awhile and were not breakfast people. Now that they were hungry, a reprise of last night's meal sounded really good to them.

In the den, others sat on the couch discussing how many friends they had in common and how they couldn't believe they hadn't met sooner. They were all so happy that they connected and couldn't wait to tell their mutual friends.

Like a ghost, I eavesdropped on the various conversations until I realized that everything I had prejudged as chaos was not at all what I perceived it to be. In my mind it was breakfast time, and everything should look a certain way. The same with the way we did our assignments. When things didn't conform to my preconceptions, I judged them as wrong. Now I saw that while things definitely were different from what I expected, nothing was actually wrong. Quite the opposite really.

In that moment I had an answer to David's question about what I had lost in my life by prejudging outcomes. A lot.

I hadn't even taken the time to meet any of the people in the den. Mr. Kripling said to meet a new person every day. I assumed he meant "a" person, not realizing I could meet more than one. That one thought caused me to realize how limited my thinking had been over the course of my life.

The scenes from the morning were gone now. What a wonderful gift I had been given to be able to go back and discover how each group's intentions were completely different from what I prejudged. How wonderful it would be to be in conversations and know exactly what was going on. Or perhaps instead, I could lose my preconceived notions and learn to appreciate the differences that are in a room at any given time.

Now I was back in the present moment. I found myself before a chair at the dining room table with Mr. Kripling and the others. The chair read, "FACING THE BATTLE." I looked around the table and sat down. Naturally the book I was supposed to read from was in front of me. Still amazed at how this happened every day, I slowly cracked the book and peeked at the pages as if I might see them blank before the words magically appeared. But that was not to be. The words were there.

Mr. Kripling asked me to begin. I considered asking why I always had to go first, but when I thought about what I had learned from my day's experience, I began to share what was on the pages of my book.

"It's not that I don't trust God," I began. "I'm afraid He's going to allow something bad to happen again. I know it will be tough, and it's scary when I go through difficult times. I know God knows what He's doing, but I'm afraid He doesn't really know what I need and that only hard times lie ahead.

"I don't see myself benefiting from anything extraordinary in my life. Great things only happen to others because He likes them better. I'm at the point of believing that if something bad happens, it's just easier to blame God. Even so, I accept that He does know the bigger picture, and I only see what's happening in this moment."

I knew dinner was to be served, but after hearing what I just read and thinking about the day's events, I needed to be alone. I excused myself and went to my room in a bit of a daze. It was getting dark now, and as I came to the top of the stairs, I could see light in my room.

Was someone in there? I knew I hadn't left the light on because I had not needed it that morning. I cautiously approached my room, listening for anyone who might be there. Could someone be trying to steal my treasures? It was probably Mary wanting her book back. If so, what should I say to her?

I slowed my steps even more and peeked around the entryway to my room. No one was there, but there was a small table with a lavender cloth on it. Upon entering, I saw the source of the light. On the table were lit candles, a plate of food and two movie tickets. Dinner and a movie, how funny.

Looking at the plate of fettuccine alfredo, I became very hungry and sat down to enjoy my meal. At first I thought one of the servants must have seen what a difficult day I had and set this up for me. But how could they know I wasn't going to eat dinner with the rest of the visitors? I myself knew only a moment ago.

When I sat in the chair a well-known presence came over me.

"Kris, Kris, are you there?"

I knew he had been there. Maybe it was my gift kicking in, but I somehow knew he had been there. Had he set this up for me? Was this his way of cheering me on? What was I really doing here, and why did I all of sudden feel so uncomfortable at the thought of Kris putting together this candle-lit dinner with the movie tickets?

For Kris to have done this meant that I was obviously important to him. The thought of my being important was difficult. For me to be important to Kris was improbable, but even more uncomfortable.

CHAPTER 8

Unworthy

I finished my tasty meal, kissed my movie tickets and tucked away my treasures. Then I bounced into the bathroom to wash my face and get ready for bed. The thought of Kris's leaving this treat for me was so sweet, and yet there was that nagging discomfort.

As I looked in the mirror, I saw a reflection of pajamas hanging on the back of the bathroom door. They appeared to be a pale shade of green, ever so slight but noticeable against the whiteness of the door.

I was reluctant to take off the pale pink dress, but I then figured I would be trading it for something else with color. I pulled on the pajamas and climbed into bed, giving my beautifully set table another glance. My duvet was no longer a solid pale pink. Shades of green shot through it as well. Not my favorite combination, I thought to myself, but it works.

Hidden!

As soon as I pulled the covers over me, I experienced a sense of exhilaration combined with calm. Two contrasting senses, yet there was peace in the room. The curtain billowed gently in the night air. And through the window, I saw a star twinkle as my eyes closed.

As the fourth day dawned, I woke with reluctance because I had dreamt of my sweet, beautiful girls back home. They were doing their school work and playing games with Kris. It was so soothing that I did not want to leave. With Kris's presence from the night before and the realness of my dream, I couldn't help but be a bit homesick.

When am I going to leave this place? I wondered. Then I recalled Kim's words when we first spoke a few days ago, "We can stay as long as we like." What exactly did that mean? Could I go home now? The obvious answer seemed to be no. But why? What was keeping me here?

Analyzing the situation further, I deduced that, one, I couldn't return home because I didn't have a ride home. Two –

most disturbingly – I didn't have a way to phone Kris or someone else to pick me up. Three, if Kris was here last night, why didn't he take me home?

Anxiety raced through me as it occurred to me I might be in a nuthouse. Surely this wasn't a mental hospital. Am I crazy? Is that why I woke up here? Was I drugged so I wouldn't figure it out and put up a fight?

Rolling over to view the remains of my dinner from the previous night, I was troubled that it was gone. I threw off the covers and ran to the place where it had all been. Nothing. There was nothing here.

With my panic attack increasing, I ran to the window and looked down. Calming green grass. Instantly, rational thinking resumed. I supposed one of the servants must have come in and cleaned up in the middle of the night.

The idea of someone I didn't know entering my room while I was asleep felt like an intrusion. But I continued to calm down and get ready for the day. I began to wonder how many times I could wear my pretty pink dress before it began to smell.

As if someone were reading my mind, I saw what looked like the same style of dress. But rather than the pale pink from the day before, it was almost the color of cotton candy. I smelled it, and, just as I suspected, it was fresh and clean. Slipping out of my funky green pajamas and into my dress, I also noticed it was a bit softer than the previous one.

I have to admit, I was getting to the point where I wanted to stay awake at night to see who came into my room to make the changes in my wardrobe. Suddenly, a horrible thought entered my mind. If the remains of my lovely dinner treat from last night were gone, what about my treasures?

I ran to the drawer so hastily I hit my toe on the night stand. The pain quickly left, though, when I opened the drawer, and, to my delight, there they lay.

I finished getting ready for the day and made my way down to the kitchen. Even though I had had that big meal last evening, I was quite hungry. The smell of pancakes and bacon made me even more so.

Down the stairs I trotted expectantly, only to run into an empty room. The kitchen was empty as well, except for the amazing smell of breakfast. I then heard voices coming from the dining room. Had I overslept? Was I that late for breakfast?

I quietly approached the dining room, hoping to become invisible and not be noticed for my tardiness. Luckily, as soon as I entered the dining room I saw an empty chair at the end of the table nearest me. AMBIVALENCE.

Not sure I wanted to sit there, I tried to make myself smaller and slid into the chair hoping no one would notice. What was I thinking? Everyone must have noticed the empty chair, which meant someone was missing and that someone was me. I felt a penetrating stare but still heard the various conversations around the table. I did not want to look up to see who was staring at me. It was most likely Mary, still bitter about my having the book.

But it was my book now. Somehow I knew that it was meant for me. I slowly raised my eyes while keeping my head bowed and looked around the table. Everyone seemed to be in lively conversation. It appeared I had entered unnoticed.

With a bit of satisfaction for my sneakiness, I proceeded to help myself to the scrumptious-looking pancakes. Three should do it; I was really hungry.

Spreading the butter, I still felt someone staring at me. I raised my eyes from the task of preparing my pancakes to again scan the table. No one was paying any attention to me. Then I leaned forward to reach for the bacon, and the stare gripped me. I turned my head to the other end of the table to see Mr. Kripling.

It was an uncomfortable moment, like I had done something wrong. Our eyes locked while I was in mid-reach for my food. I thought he must have seen me try to sneak in and was trying to let me know that I hadn't gotten away with anything. I gave him a quick smile as I slowly leaned back into my seat to indulge in this yummy breakfast.

His gaze remained on me as I took the first bite. I wasn't sure if I should eat or say good morning or try to join one of the conversations. I sat there and ate as the very awkward moment continued. As enjoyable as the food was, my appetite now took a back seat to the intense look Mr. Kripling was giving me. Taking another bite, there was a sudden moment of silence. Every person stopped talking, even if they were in mid-sentence. Well, then, I thought, now they must all be staring at me. Finally, the pressure became too intense, and I threw down my fork, looked up and snapped, "WHAT!"

If ever there was a sheepish moment, this was it. It was silent because no one else was at the table except Mr. Kripling, sitting at the other end of the table, and me. Sinking back into my chair, my immediate thoughts were, where did everyone go and how did they all disappear in an instant?

Mr. Kripling cocked one eyebrow and said, "Nice dress."

Glancing at my dress and back at him, I noticed for the first time since coming to Vic'tim Mentala that Mr. Kripling's white suit had black pearl buttons. I replied to his compliment with a thank you and, not knowing what to do, kept eating.

"Do you know why you're here?"

Mr. Kripling's formerly soothing voice now boomed. I thought for a moment that a better question is, how does time seem to stop in this place?

"To get better?"

"You don't seem so sure, Michelle. Are you sure?"

Another moment passed. Was I sure? "Yes, I am sure."

"Better from what?"

"Well, you know, my past."

"How can anyone make their past better?"

More questions. Why was everyone here so full of questions? Moreover, why do they think I have the answers? I supposed I should play along. After all, he did pull that exceptional disappearing act. It was rather remarkable that no one could hear our conversation.

"I suppose no one can make their past better," I said. "I have never thought of it like that."

"Do you know why you are here?"

Now I thought a bit longer. If it wasn't about my past, then why *was* I here? I had to admit, I was stumped. For what seemed a duration of five or ten minutes, I thought while Mr. Kripling sat there waiting for the answer. The length of time that passed in silence didn't seem to bother him.

Then I remembered the book in my room. "*WHO YOU CHOOSE TO BE.*" It took a few minutes, but finally I found my answer, and this time gave it with a bit of pride in my voice. "To figure out my future."

"Are you confident?"

Suddenly the room was again alive with voices as Mr. Kripling's soothing tone returned. "Today you will meet someone new."

He got up from his chair and strolled back toward the kitchen. The servants scurried over to clear the table, as if Mr. Kripling's departure were their cue to clean up. I looked around to see who I might be drawn to today.

There was Mary, her eyes a wild red tint and her clothing a simple pair of slacks with a buttoned-down, collared shirt and a scarf covering her hair.

With her hair covered, her white outfit made her skin appear even more pale than before.

Getting up from the table, I noticed Jamie, still giddy as ever, her frilly dress definitely reflecting her personality except for its barely beige color.

David was now gone, which I somehow expected. Everyone had gotten up from the table and seemed to be in conversation already.

There were eleven of us, Mr. Kripling being the twelfth, so if ten people paired up each day, someone would be alone. I supposed today that meant me.

Then a lovely thought came to mind. I could sneak outside, run in the grass and indulge in the beauty of the landscape. I also remembered seeing a maze from my bedroom window. Perhaps I could see if I could conquer it.

Out of the blue, I felt like a child again. Leaving my seat, again trying to avoid attention, I walked toward the back door while everyone else was engrossed in their conversations. I let out a little giggle for no apparent reason and headed for the maze.

Then I saw something that didn't belong. Or, I should say, someone. In the rose garden on the way to the maze was a pond surrounded by benches. Seated on one of the benches was a little girl.

She couldn't have been more than seven years old, the same age as Lisa.

Although there was something eerily recognizable about her, to my disappointment she was not Lisa. She was wearing a little denim jumper and red turtleneck. Her flowing light brown hair glistened in the sunlight as she swirled her toes in the grass.

Then it struck me. Her clothing was so colorful, the deep red and the blue in the jumper. I had become so accustomed to seeing white, with maybe a splash of pale color here and there, that her clothing jolted me. But then, we were outside where everything was magnificently colorful.

Even though she obviously belonged amid this beauty, there was a sense of grief about her.

As I moved toward her, she didn't even acknowledge my presence.

I thought back to the scene in the dining room when everyone disappeared and left me alone with Mr. Kripling. Was this a mirage?

I took a deep breath and gently sat down next to the little girl, trying not to startle her. After all, I was a stranger.

Curious about what she was doing there and thinking perhaps her parents were inside, I tried to strike up a conversation.

"Waiting for your mom or dad?"

"Nope!" she said without hesitation.

Not knowing what to say next, but feeling obligated to continue the conversation and find out about her parents, I asked, "What are you doing?"

"Thinking."

Now we were getting somewhere. "What about?"

"No one ever explains anything to me."

Whoa, I wasn't expecting that, but I could certainly relate to it.

"What would you like to know? Maybe I can help."

"Well, I was never taught morals. I'm expected to figure out the difference between right and wrong all by myself. It's as if I'm supposed to know stuff without anyone actually teaching me anything."

She looked to be seven, nine at the oldest, and she was worried about being taught morals?

"Well, you're still a little young. Maybe your parents haven't thought about it."

"Oh, please."

For the first time, she lifted her head and glanced at me. "When I started my period, I knew nothing about it. No one ever explained what was going on or why this was happening. I was instantly supposed to know all about it. How was I supposed to know?"

Was she really talking about her menstrual cycle? Maybe she is closer to nine years old.

"Wait! What? No one ever explained to you about your menstrual cycle?"

"Nope."

No wonder she's out here looking so gloomy. How awful to be all alone with nobody to clue her in about simple things, let alone something so essential. Gosh, should I tell her?

"Obviously, I figured it out, but why should I have to? My parents never taught me that drugs were bad for me and not to do them or warned me how drinking alcohol could distort my thinking. Or what about waiting until I'm married to have sex? That would have been a useful piece of information."

This was getting bizarre, and I was becoming officially freaked out by what was coming out of this little girl's mouth. I was positive she was no older than nine. Why was she concerned with such things at such a young age? How did she know about these things if there was no one to give her information?

Before I could ask, she continued: "My feelings are never acknowledged. I'm the only girl in my family, so no one understands me. My brothers think I'm spoiled, so I can't talk to them about anything of substance. All we do is fight. My parents are always working, and my mom never offers any female support."

Her words penetrated my mind, and my heart began to ache. I thought back to my own childhood and knew exactly how she felt. As I listened to her, astonished at the similarities of our situations, I couldn't help but be concerned.

"My mom never taught me etiquette and barely touched on manners," she continued. "I don't know what it means to be a lady.

"She buys me clothes and thinks she's doing such a nice thing for me, but often I don't even like them. She never asks me what I like. She buys what she likes and then accuses me of being ungrateful when I don't get excited about them. I don't dare ask her to exchange them, so I have to wear clothes I can't stand. It's embarrassing and I feel like everyone is making fun of me."

Again it all seemed so familiar and I wondered if she would grow up caring so much about what others thought of her that it would dictate who she was. The flood gates were opened now as she kept unloading her innermost feelings.

"My parents buy me things to show me their love instead of expressing it with words or affection. If I barely express that I like this or that, they buy it for me, even if I tell them I don't really want it. If only they would give me a hug or say 'I love you.'"

That was it! My heart completely broke open. Who were these parents? I felt a sudden burst of deep compassion for this precious little thing. I saw a scared and confused little girl. Her story was heartbreaking. I yearned to nurture her and make everything better in her little life. She deserved much better.

With tears welling in my eyes, I embraced the little girl with the strange familiarities. Rocking her in my arms, I gave her the hug she longed for. And though I did not know who she was or where she came from, I was compelled to let this valuable little girl hear the words she so desired. "I love you. I love you so very much."

After sitting with her for what seemed like an hour, rocking and holding her as she wept in my arms, I opened my eyes to see how she was doing. My arms were wrapped around my knees, which were pulled into my chest, and I wondered what happened to the little girl who was so desperate for love and understanding.

It didn't take long to figure out why I identified so much with this little girl. I understood now that I was blaming that powerless little child for everything I didn't like about my adult life. I even looked down on her with disdain because of her weaknesses.

No longer were the child and the adult separate. I could protect her as an adult, and I would no longer hold her accountable for anything that happened to her at a young age, or any age for that matter. She was just a little girl!

I took a deep breath as I realized how special that little girl was to have survived all that had been thrown at her.

She was very courageous and deserved a healthier life. No longer holding her responsible, I felt I could walk with my head held high and no longer feel embarrassed or want for anything. I could actually see myself being able to participate in a life of abundance, no longer lacking in any area of my life.

As I sat there, for the first time I observed my surroundings. This is a peculiar place. The garden was full of vitality. There were roses of every color imaginable and even some colors I'd never seen before. It was mesmerizing.

Then I remembered where I was heading when I encountered the little girl. With renewed vigor, I turned toward the maze.

Skipping along to my destination, I happened to look up at the castle and see the window to my room. The curtain gently moving in the breeze appeared to be almost lavender. But as it blew, it appeared pink and then green. The pastel colors flickered back and forth as the breeze caught the curtain. How creative, I thought. This place

seemed to have surprises around every corner and at any moment in time.

I thought I was ready to take up the challenge of the maze when a feeling of worthlessness hit me. It was as if I had no value, and only those who were valued could pass through the maze. Was the maze speaking to me? No, it was not the maze itself but something on the other side that drove me back to the castle.

My determined demeanor dissipated and I dropped to my knees. Hopelessness engulfed me. I could not set foot in the maze. Only a certain type of person was capable of entering. It was not to be, not today, and possibly not ever.

Was this my destiny? Would I ever make it back home? Kim's words when I first arrived rang out again, "You can stay as long as you like." I don't agree. I don't want to be here and yet I'm stuck. I can't leave; I can't choose whether I stay or go.

What happened? What changed from the moment I felt victory over protecting my inner child to defeat at the entrance of the maze? I got up and drug my feet back to the castle, entering the back door without hesitation. I didn't care whether anyone took notice of my having been outside. This was where I belonged.

Still feeling down, I saw one of the servants taking bowls of soup to the dining table, and I headed that way. Glancing at my chair I read, "STAGES OF ABUSE." Yes, this was fitting, considering my day and the roller coaster of emotions I had experienced.

I was happy for a light dinner because I didn't have much of an appetite. I looked at Mr. Kripling, and his eyes locked on mine. "Did you meet someone new today," he asked?

Then I remembered what he said before we parted ways after breakfast, "Today you will meet someone new." Once again I assumed that I knew the outcome and that it would be someone from the table I had not yet met. When will I learn? Don't assume; keep an open mind.

At least it no longer bothered me when things didn't go according to how I assumed they would or thought they should. It's refreshing, even exhilarating, to experience someone else's thought process or point of view. It's almost adventurous. Boy, this place is causing an emotional train wreck.

Glancing back at Mr. Kripling, I saw he was still waiting for my answer. "Actually, I did."

He gave me a nod and continued eating.

Everyone seemed eager to share tonight. Not having been inside during the day, I had no idea what occurred or where all the excitement was coming from. Then I observed two new people at the table. No matter who came and went, there were always eleven of us, mostly women.

Now I saw that the excitement was over handsome male twins sitting on either side of Mr. Kripling.

Mr. Kripling caught my eye and gave me another nod, which I took as a sign to again be the first to share. The servants quickly replaced our empty soup bowls with our books. Having become accustomed to the book with my writing in it, I opened to the appropriate page.

###

"I always wanted to be someone else and in someone else's family. I always knew I could do certain things and had certain gifts but was never given the opportunity to make the most of my gifts or talents. I always thought I could do anything, really. However, there was no one to encourage me in any way. No one else believed in me. Finally, I couldn't do it alone anymore. With no encouragement, only discouragement, I lost interest and settled for less in everything I did. It didn't take long to figure out I wasn't good enough; I'm just average in every way. Sometimes, a glimmer of great potential would rise to the surface, but I dared not bring that potential out in the open."

The others shared eagerly, clearly showing off for our two new gentlemen. This is why I hate women. They become wishy-washy and phony at the drop of a hat. They will choose a guy they just met over a lifelong female friend.

And don't dare share anything too intimate with them because, should you later have a disagreement, your so-called best friend would gossip about it just to spite you.

Yep, women are pure evil. That's why I grew up hanging out with guys and have never had a great female friend. The thought of having a best girlfriend is nice, but I'm not sure it's worth the risk. I sat and half-heartedly listened to all the silliness until Mr. Kripling bid us goodnight.

He seemed to cut the evening short. He, too, must have noticed the disaster unraveling before him. Most likely there were not going to be any "aha" moments in this atmosphere.

I left my book behind, no longer wondering where it went or how it found its way back to me. It was intriguing, though, how my thoughts always ended up in the book and in my own handwriting.

My bedroom was unusually dark. Previously it was well lit by the moon. Tonight I had to feel my way to turn on the little bedside lamp. I was greeted by a surprising sight: A dozen beautiful roses stood tall on the night table next to my bed. They were the same colors I noticed earlier on the curtains but much richer shades of plum, burgundy and hunter green. I had never seen a green rose before, and it was breathtaking.

I ran my fingers over the beautiful bedding that was becoming a deeper pink. My pajamas seemed a bit darker as well. It was as if the whole room was reflecting the colors of the roses. They held the most pleasant fragrance I had ever smelled.

I bent over to smell the roses and saw a little card. I wasn't sure what to expect, maybe an encouraging word from the staff. Not an admirer, I hoped. I carefully pulled the card from the cluster of roses and hesitantly took it out of its little envelope. One thing I had learned in this place, as clichéd as it sounds, was that I never knew what to expect. The wonderful, exhilarating, precious card simply read, "I love you."

How perfect was that? I sighed. Someone here cares deeply for me. Someone here actually finds value in me. Someone here is thoughtful, kind, and generous. Of course, the only person I wanted to receive this from was Kris. With a full heart and the pain of the encounter with the little girl fading, I gazed once again at those sweet, sweet words. "I love you." I really needed to hear them.

I read them again and again because I couldn't get enough of those three words.

My spirit was so needy for affection that these roses and the words on the card seemed to quench my thirsty soul.

As I read the card again, I heard a voice saying those same words right into my ear. I quickly turned to see who it was, but no one was there. "Kris, Kris, is that you?"

No answer. But I was certain I heard an actual voice whisper those words to me.

"God? Jesus? Is that You?"

Without knowing for sure who left the roses and the card or whose voice I heard, I let it rest and contented myself with the idea that someone thought enough of me to buy these remarkable roses. And whoever it was knew those simple words were exactly what I needed to hear. For me, that's all that mattered now.

I smiled at my colorful pajamas and at how alive my room was becoming. Could a person change the atmosphere so much that it would manifest itself in beautiful colors? What an inspiring thought! However, exploring that thought would have to wait until tomorrow. Emotionally drained from the long, arduous day, I climbed into bed and pretended it was Kris who left the roses and whispered those perfect words.

CHAPTER 9

Self-Contempt

As I fell asleep, memories of the day ran through my mind, especially the feelings triggered by my conversation with the little girl. Her pain still infiltrated my heart.

That night my subconscious went to a cutting place deep within. It was the kind of dream that was so realistic I actually thought I was awake. The little girl I met in the garden earlier that day – me, Little Michelle – was playing with my two girls, Lisa and Jill. The girls seemed to want the same toy Little Michelle was playing with, and they chided her, "C'mon, Michelle. You're supposed to share."

But Little Michelle loved that toy dearly and was afraid that if she shared, it would get broken. She resolved not to part with it.

Suddenly, Lisa and Jill had reinforcements. At least five other children all wanted the toy. Some would try to coerce it from Little Michelle; others tried to trick her into giving it up, and yet others promised her an even nicer toy in exchange. I could not understand why they were so desperate for this particular toy. What was so significant about it? Was it the toy itself or the fact that Little Michelle had it and they didn't? I pondered this while watching the dream unfold like it was a scene on television. Lisa and Jill were the first to walk away, no longer wanting the toy. But the others were persistent and began to wear down Little Michelle. She was becoming weak and no longer had the will to resist.

She began to rationalize that sharing the toy would be okay. Maybe, just maybe, they would treat it nicely and sharing wouldn't be as bad as she anticipated. She reluctantly gave the toy to these children, convinced they were her new friends. To my horror, they took it and ran, throwing Little Michelle into turmoil and causing her to feel like an easy target for cruelty. I watched as Little Michelle began to upbraid herself.

"You're such an idiot! You knew you shouldn't have shared your toy. You knew something bad would happen. Why are you so stupid? When are you ever going to get some brains and use them?"

She began to sob uncontrollably, wondering if she would ever get her toy back. Picking herself up, Little Michelle proceeded along a narrow dirt road. As she wandered down the road, she met many people. Known for being gullible, she believed and trusted everything people told her – especially if they seemed to care.

She became a virtual slave to anyone who showed even a hint of concern for her. Even if she knew the person was insincere, at least she could pretend. That was better than facing the fact that no one cared for her.

Little Michelle discovered that a lot of people would lie and use her. When she couldn't continue to give them what they wanted, they dumped her back by the dirt road and walked away.

Blaming herself, she was convinced she should have done whatever they wanted so as not to have been left alone again on the deserted road.

The next time around, she resolved to do just that, go along with whatever anyone wanted. But the result was still the same. Ultimately, she was dumped back by the road and could only watch as her would-be friends walked away.

No matter what she did or didn't do, Little Michelle couldn't seem to make anyone care about her.

During that moment, all alone, walking along the abandoned dirt road, she remembered her precious toy.

Not only had it been stolen from her but her soul had been taken with it – taken piece by piece by each person who entered her life.

It became crystal clear why she wasn't important enough to be valued, and in that moment, she realized something was wrong with her.

She was like a wounded animal on protective guard. She felt vulnerable because of the pain but unwilling to let anyone help. As she continued down the path, she no longer allowed anyone to come close to her.

As the dream progressed, Little Michelle continued to grow in years and become callous to friends, losing many in the process. Because she was always so distant, no one could ever love her or even put up with her for very long.

The pain of rejection caused her to feel like an awful human being. She was trying to be the best person she could be, but it still wasn't enough for people to love her.

As I continued the TV-like dream, Little Michelle's feelings once again became my own. She was a prisoner in my own body, damaged goods nobody wanted.

I felt contempt for Michelle because she would not fight and continued to be a prisoner instead of escaping or engaging in the battle. I desired to be in control and have everything a certain way. It repulsed me that Michelle had no control.

The dream ended with her lying on the ground in despair, dirty and shackled from years of abuse, in a cold cement chamber, weeping, with no way out.

I was awakened by the tears rolling down my face. How I got here was finally beginning to make sense. The light of day pressed against my face, and I knew what I had to do. I turned to the night table for the book with blank pages I had taken from Mary only a short time ago. At last I was beginning to achieve some self-awareness and I needed to write about it.

To my horror, as one nightmare ended, another one began. The book was gone. In panic, I sat on the edge of the bed and desperately looked through the drawer. This did not make any sense. All my treasures were there but the book. I fell to the floor searching every inch beneath the bed. Nothing! I ran to the bathroom, in a frenzy looking for it.

The dream had caused me to be aware of so many areas of my life as well as my continuing self-destructive thought processes. I finally had something to illustrate, something in my life that was significant, and no place to acknowledge it. The book was the key.

As the anger welled up in my throat I began to call myself, names. "Stupid idiot. How could you have misplaced the book? You knew the book was significant. You should have taken precautions."

I feared where the book might be or, worse, who may have it. Through my tears, I heard a loud commotion downstairs. The distraction restored my sanity.

Reaching for a pen, I began to write on a pad that had been on the nightstand since I arrived.

Dear God,

I've noticed that I put my trust and value in people. I've also been teaching my girls some of these same values. I'm sorry I didn't realize what I was doing. Help me to turn things around and care more about what You think.

Sometimes I become irritated with You, and most of the time I feel sad that I have looked at You as this awful person who wants to see me fail. Help me to see You for who You really are and show others the same, especially, my girls.

I desperately need You to help me show my girls more love. Help me to understand them and to be more patient with them no matter the circumstance. And remind me to not be so serious all the time. Show me what to say to them and give me the courage to respond to their love with Your love. Help me to be a better mother, friend, wife, and daughter of Yours, Father God."

Thank you,

Michelle

CHAPTER 10

Blaming Others

If I thought my dream had been revelatory, it was just as well that I didn't know what the day had in store for me.

Another loud crash downstairs again refocused me. Wise now to the fact that even items in one's room are not necessarily off limits, my love note to God went under my mattress.

Eager to see what all the fuss was about, I rapidly cleaned myself up. Straightening my bed, I briefly took in the more vivid multicolored hues on my duvet. I couldn't focus on the color change at the moment, as interesting as it was. My concentration was on the clamoring below.

Throwing on my dress, a great deal brighter in color as well, I left the room. I came to a halt at the top of the stairs. Instead of the expected chaos, there was complete silence.

Clearly, there had been a commotion. But now, looking down the stairs, all I saw was Jamie. She was sitting at the bottom of the steps, her head buried in her knees. Her body language spoke an obvious discontent. I walked down the stairs in a tentative manner, not knowing what to expect. Jamie's previous white tank top and shorts were now a light shade of peach.

Jamie was in an extreme emotional state as her body jerked with deep sobbing. Something awful had happened here. I carefully sat down next to her. I don't know why I did because on previous occasions Jamie seemed a bit naïve, and I really didn't want anything to do with her.

In an instant, that all changed. Something came over me. Was that compassion? Maybe I could give her a chance and see if there was anything I could do.

After all, she was a mess, and it didn't seem that anyone else was coming to her rescue. In fact the castle was an empty silence.

With a gentle touch I pulled Jamie's hair away from her face and began to experiment with this compassionate state.

"What happened, Jamie? Are you okay?"

She mumbled through her tears, "What do you care? Since when do you care about anyone other than yourself?"

Ouch! That stung. Here I am trying to lend a helping hand and I get slapped in the face. This is the very reason I don't get involved with people and confirmed my reasoning for not befriending women.

I began evaluating how this might turn out and whether it was worth the effort. Tempted to get up and walk away, a force kept me glued to the seat next to her.

"Are you just curious and want something to gossip about, or do you really care?" she asked.

Oh man, I was getting hammered. Where was this coming from? Here she is accusing me of the very thing I accuse other women of. Maybe she's not as naïve as I thought. When I thought about it, it was a pretty accurate read. She had every right to doubt my sincerity.

"I really want to help," I said. "I won't say anything to anyone."

There, I had reached out to her, even in the face of her criticism. I didn't answer her question, but it made me ponder. Was reaching out to Jamie truly an act of

161

compassion or was her assessment correct that I was just curious?

I decided the answer was both. I came to terms with the fact that, yes, I was curious. But at the same time, I really did feel bad for her. After all, most people don't cry without reason.

Jamie then told me that she had discovered a book with her name on it. "I was upstairs exploring one of the hallways when I discovered these magnificent French doors leading outside to a balcony. I pass this way every morning, but it had never occurred to me to explore any part of the castle.

"Yesterday, I happened to glance down the hallway and it was as if the outdoors beckoned to me. I was curious, so I followed the urge and moved with haste in that direction. As I passed by the doors to the balcony and glanced their way, a white flash caught my eye. There on the balcony was a white book, which I assumed someone had dropped. So I went out on to the balcony to retrieve it."

"You went outside?"

"Of course, the book was outside. What does that matter?"

"Remember? We're not allowed to go outside."

"What are you talking about? Do you want to know what's wrong or not?"

"Yeah, yeah. Sorry, I got distracted when you told me you went outside." She doesn't know about not going outside. Did Mary lie to me when she told me that?

"I opened the book to see if there was a name inside to identify it, and when I did, I saw that it was mine."

"Excuse me?"

"It was mine; it had my name in it. Only I don't remember ever having that book."

"And?"

"I was stunned and a little freaked out, so I took it back to my room and put it in my night table drawer. I didn't have time to explore it further and wasn't sure I wanted to, so I left it there until I had the courage to do so.

"Last night I had a weird and wonderful dream. When I woke up, I had an epiphany and wanted to write about it in the book."

She paused and almost started crying again. I was dying to ask about the dream but decided to pursue it later and focus on the book.

"Jamie? What about the book?"

"It's missing. But who would have taken it? Who even knew about it? I didn't even know about it. Was I imagining things? I seem to imagine things a lot in this place. Do you think the book is real, or do you think I imagined it? Because if I knew I had imagined it, I would feel a whole lot better."

Oh, here we go, Miss Naïve just showed up.

"No, no the book is definitely real. But you say your name was in it?"

Her eyes now welling up again, with a crack in her voice she confirmed it: "Uh huh."

So there is more than one of these books. Does everyone have one?

It was truly strange that we both had odd, yet meaningful, dreams last night. But because I was more curious about the book, I continued to probe.

"What are you doing down here? I heard a big commotion and that's what led me to you."

She said she had been intent on finding the book, so she began a search of the castle. She was downstairs moving furniture, looking in every drawer, which must have caused all the noise I heard when I discovered my book was gone as well.

Then I remembered where I got my book. Or was it even my book? Did I steal Mary's book? Mine did not have my name in it. I satisfied my thoughts with the fact that I was meant to discover it when I saw Mary looking at it. I took it because it was mine to take.

How did I know that? Where did that thought even come from? It was almost like an inner voice, not mine, told me the truth.

With my attention back on Jamie, I asked her where she last saw her book.

"Did you ever take it from your room?"

"Well, yes. When I awoke, I took the book from the night table. I wasn't sure I wanted to look inside again, so I set it down while I got cleaned up.

"Then I finally decided it was only a book and there was no need to be afraid. I always get up way before breakfast is ready, so I took the book to the kitchen, made myself a cup of tea and sat in the den like I always do.

I was in the den looking at the photos in the book, which seemed somehow familiar. I set it down and went back to the kitchen for some sweetener, and when I got back, it was gone."

Her book has pictures?

"Was anyone in the den with you?"

"Well, yeah, but why would anyone want to take my book?"

"Who was in the den?"

Before I even asked the question, I knew the answer. A small voice spoke the name into my head, and it dropped from my mouth. "Mary."

She opened her mouth wide. "Yep, how did you know?"

Then it occurred to me that she could have taken my book as well. Again, more questions came to mind. First of all, why would she want our books?

"Did you ask Mary if she had seen your book?"

"No, she wasn't there when I got back. As soon as I saw the book wasn't where I left it, I began frantically searching.

"I became frustrated and ran out of the den not knowing where to search next. I sat down on the steps and started to cry, and that's when you found me."

So what to do? Should we confront Mary or should we talk to Mr. Kripling? Though he was only around at mealtime, it was obvious he was in charge.

"What do you want to do, Jamie? How can I help?"

"I don't know. It will probably turn up. Don't worry about it."

Don't worry about it? I don't know about her, but I want my book back. I wasn't sure what the day had in store, but what I did know was that I was going to find my book.

Jamie headed off, and as she left, I again noticed her clothing. There was definitely a shade of peach in her outfit. I found a smile on my face, though I wasn't sure why. Seeing the color made me happy.

As a matter of fact, seeing all the shades of color on the various clothes and in my room and outside was beginning to fill me with happiness. I couldn't say why; they just did.

CHAPTER 11

Settling for Less

Getting up from the stairs, I turned around and ran right into Mary – literally. Her face was so white, she looked ill. I had to ask, "Are you feeling all right?"

"Why would you even ask that?"

What do I say to that? Because you look like crap?

"You just look a little tired," I said. She moved passed me, and I couldn't help but see that even her lips were white. Something was definitely wrong with that girl.

Then I remembered the missing books and turned around to call out to her. But as suddenly as she appeared, she was gone. There one minute and gone the next. So far this day is turning out to be a peculiar one.

With my stomach growling, I headed to the kitchen. Odd! There was no one there. I went to the dining table and, sure enough, that's where everyone was. The only seat left was directly to Mr. Kripling's right. There would be no sneaking in today.

Glancing down I read only one word on the chair, "SHAME."

I reached for the fruit directly in front of me and began listening to what was happening at the table. Mr. Kripling was talking about doing things a little differently today.

He explained that most of us had already encountered a situation that morning and that we were going to share now rather than wait until the end of the day. He seemed to know everything that happened in this place, even if he couldn't witness it all first hand. It's almost as if he had spies who reported to him. Then a thought occurred to me: What if the place is bugged? What if there are hidden cameras? Before I became too paranoid, I decided that wasn't his style. But it was curious how situations in the castle were well-known to him. And not only the circumstances, but the details.

When he finished speaking, I looked down at my plate and there was my book. Looking up at Mr. Kripling, he gazed back with a nod of his head and said, "You may proceed."

I was used to going first, so it no longer bothered me. I began to read what had been written on the pages.

"I was stupid enough to fall prey to him. I was gullible and didn't know any better. I believed him. Now that I'm older, I dislike being tricked into believing something as part of someone's joke. It causes me to become disappointed in myself and treat myself with contempt. Then I withdraw and treat them with contempt until they feel uncomfortable and leave. I can release my anger on myself and no one gets hurt. When others are involved, the contempt will push them away from me and penalize them for invading my space. There are only a few people I feel comfortable with. Mainly I'd rather not deal with people."

I put down my book.

"How does this relate to the encounter you had today?"

Who was Mr. Kripling talking to? Every eye was on me, including his.

"What?"

"Remember the announcement I made a moment ago that you were going to share about an encounter you had today. How does this relate to the encounter?"

Oh, why did he always have to change everything? Does he really want me to talk about my encounter with Jamie? That is so unorthodox, not to mention an invasion of privacy. Sharing this would ruin everything. I didn't want to expose anything regarding the books. And I certainly didn't want Mary to know I was on to her. Maybe I could do it without revealing the whole episode.

As I thought about what had taken place earlier, Jamie's words returned with a sting. I gave Mr. Kripling the condensed version.

"When I offered to help Jamie with a problem, she asked why I wanted to help. She said I hadn't cared before, so why the sudden concern."

Hearing those words spoken out loud caused me to make the connection with what I just read, and it was heart-wrenching. I'm a rude person. I act that way to protect myself. Never before had I seen that as being selfish. To me it was survival.

Then the attention passed to the person next to me. I finished my fruit and listened to the others.

###

In the middle of the sharing, I noticed a strange thing. A man was sitting on the living room couch. I had no idea how long he had been sitting there. I felt all that was shared at the table was personal and wasn't anyone else's business. Was this stranger listening to everything? How did he get in the castle and why was he here? He seemed to be waiting for someone.

Everyone shared, and no one said anything about the visitor in the living room. Didn't they care whether an outsider heard their innermost thoughts? Who did this man remind me of? He was definitely an older gentleman, at least in his sixties or seventies.

Perhaps he was visiting one of his children here and was waiting for us to finish our breakfast and sharing. What struck me was that not one person at the table acknowledged him. I started to feel bad for him sitting there all alone.

I don't believe I really had a relationship with my father. I don't remember ever having a meaningful conversation with him. He spoke to me only to tell me to do some chore, to punish me for something, or when he and my mom were going somewhere.

My father seemed uninterested in what was happening in my life or how I felt about anything. He basically shut me out of his world. All I heard from him was criticism. He did not have an open mind. He expected things to be his way without compromise.

It was quite clear, if I had a problem, it was my problem. There was no lending an ear, no input or advice.

Far from offering a safe haven, I thought only about my father to wonder what punishment I was going to get or what negative thing he was going to say.

Looking up, I saw the couch in the living room was filling up. Now an elderly woman sat next to the man. Most likely parents, they must have come here to visit their son or daughter.

Again my mind drifted to my own parents. My mother did not offer any female support. I was the only girl in my family – five boys and me. I could not depend on her for strength or direction. She was not a good role model; no hugs or kisses that I could remember past the age of four.

I did not feel protected by her because she failed to teach me anything. I had to learn almost everything on my own, and because of that, I made a lot of mistakes. She was never home, always working. Money and buying things were more important than being there emotionally. But if you don't have it, you can't give it.

As I sat there in a stupor, my childhood came rushing back to me, along with memories of those horrible nights of being assaulted. Because my parents were so inattentive, I did not know I could stop the assaults. I was denied real options because I didn't know I had any.

I couldn't tell my parents. The only real time we spent together was when they took the whole family somewhere they wanted to go. When we went on vacation, instead of real family fun, they would throw in a few activities for the kids out of obligation.

There was no one for me to turn to. The helplessness was overwhelming. No one came to check on me at night to make sure I was all right. If either of my parents had taken the time to peek in on me, none of it would have happened.

I was so scared and confused that I didn't realize I could have told my brother "No!" The idea of having a choice didn't enter my mind.

"Missing something?" Mary said, interrupting my thoughts.

I was taken aback by her pasty white face.

"I noticed you seemed a bit miffed when I saw you on the stairs this morning," she said.

Before engaging with Mary, I looked to see who had gone to visit with the elderly couple, but they were no longer there.

"Yes, as a matter of fact, I am missing something," I said. "What would you know about it?"

"Enough to know that you're not going to do anything about it."

Did she just call me a coward? As she turned and skipped off after Mr. Kripling, I felt the jab of her words. Such a cruel day – first Jamie and now Mary. But I couldn't deny their words. I don't challenge myself or try to succeed at anything that doesn't seem easy.

But never having had any support or education about much of life and never having had positive influences, how could I succeed?

And an even better question, why would God not want me to succeed? Why all the hindrances?

CHAPTER 12

Betrayal

I felt like I had been through an emotional meat grinder. It had been a strange day in a strange place. I took stock of all that happened during my time in Vic'tim Mentala. The people here were all nice enough, though it was maddening the way everything constantly changed.

Then it struck me: Each person here has a story of being involved in some type of abuse. That is the common thread.

We all started out wearing white clothing, but then our clothing began to transform to beautiful reds, pinks, greens, blues, etc., depending on the person. What caused that? Was it our growing self-discovery? Mary is the only one who is, in fact, getting whiter.

The colors must have emerged through inner healing.

Mysteries remained, however. I no longer saw David. Had he gotten caught going out the front door and not been allowed to return? A few times I noticed others going out the front door, which I thought was a bold statement, considering the rules.

But even I had, against my nature, ventured outside and enjoyed the vision of the beautiful mountains and pond. The freshness cleared my head, and I had the insightful conversation with Little Michelle.

Then there was Mr. Kripling. What was his story, I wondered. Is he a psychiatrist of some sort? Come to think of it, I knew nothing about him other than this must be his place.

Usually, when someone came to speak at church or at a retreat, they told a little about themselves to show proficiency and gain credibility. Not so with Mr. Kripling, though I admit the authority he exudes speaks for itself.

The dining table was now empty. I wondered where everyone had gone and what we were intended to do. We had already shared. Was I still expected to meet someone new? We had not been given any instructions.

Hidden!

I passed the study where Mary and I had our first encounter and heard familiar voices. My back pressing into the wall, I leaned around to peek through the crack in the door where the hinge and door post connected. Just as I thought, it was Mary and Mr. Kripling.

They spoke in quiet voices, and I couldn't quite make out what they were saying. What caught my eye, though, making me no longer interested in the conversation, was the open desk drawer holding several of the white books.

They were exactly like the one that was gone from my room. Though they all looked the same, they seemed somehow different in a way I couldn't put my finger on. But I did know my suspicions about Mary were correct.

A tap on my shoulder caused me to jump and let out a gasp. I spun around to see Jamie.

"What are you doing? Whatcha lookin' at?"

"Shhh."

Hoping Mary and Mr. Kripling didn't hear me or Jamie, I led her away from the den.

"I was looking for someone new to talk to, and I thought maybe I saw your book."

She yelled out excitedly, "You saw my book?"

If they hadn't heard us before, they definitely had now. In a quick, but firm fashion, I maneuvered Jamie back down the hallway to the kitchen, motioning her to keep her voice low.

"I'm not sure, but maybe, yes."

"Where?"

"I don't want to say. You're going to have to trust me on this one. I want to make sure it's your book before I say anything."

I hoped that satisfied her. Otherwise, she could ruin everything. I didn't have a plan quite yet, but one was beginning to form. She looked at me for a minute, and with a slow, drawn-out drawl said, "Okay."

Then she rushed off as if she were late for an appointment. That is one person who can go from hot to cold in an instant, I thought.

In the meantime, I stood in the kitchen pondering why all those books were in the desk drawer. Were Mary and Mr. Kripling in cahoots? I thought he was one of the good guys. As a sense of betrayal began to set in, I wasn't sure what to think of him, but it was clear that Mary was here to sabotage any progress anyone made during their stay.

Feeling the need for a safe, quiet place, I sprinted up to my room as fast as my feet would carry me. Out of breath, I stormed in and slammed the door behind me, falling to my knees as tears filled my eyes. Resentment rose inside me. I was angry. I threw myself on the bed and tears flooded my pillow. I wanted to go home. How did I get to this place?

When I woke up it was dark, and I realized I must have fallen asleep. The events of the day came rushing back, and once again the feeling of betrayal raged inside me. I turned on the lamp and, to my amazement, sitting on the night table was an arrangement of fruit. The scrumptious treat included pineapple rings, strawberries, cantaloupe, honeydew, bananas, and grapes, all placed on long sticks in a beautiful arrangement. One of the servants must have noticed my absence at the table and was kind enough to bring this beautiful bouquet of fruit.

I began eating and realized I had never tasted strawberries so sweet or grapes so juicy. Next, I tried the pineapple, equally as juicy and sweet. Where did they get this fruit out here in the mountains? While I ate, I began to plot my revenge against Mary. I needed to get her to admit taking the books in front of a witness. I was really surprised that no one else noticed how pasty white she was becoming. It was clear to me now, she wasn't one of us. There had to be some evidence of her taking the books.

Feeling a sudden sleepiness, I popped one last strawberry into my mouth and curled up in bed without even getting into my pajamas or washing my face.

Daylight broke through my curtain, but no sunshine, only a brisk breeze. The dark cloudy sky mocked the day, and it looked like rain.

The cool air made me shiver. My duvet was now a beautiful purple, green, blue, and, of course, pink. I was happy to see linen pants and a long-sleeved pink shirt draped over the chair. Someone must have looked at the forecast. I have to say the servants here are very thoughtful. They even discarded my half-eaten fruit bouquet.

The new clothes warmed my body, and I felt myself become more at ease.

Yet I still felt betrayed as I wondered how to handle Mr. Kripling and Mary. The truth was that I didn't know what they were up to or why those books were in that drawer. I simply knew their behavior was unethical. I wasn't sure how to conduct myself when I encountered them.

Quite frankly, it was safer to act nice and let the struggles rage within. Reluctant to make my way downstairs, I decided I couldn't hide in my room forever – although the thought did occur to me.

Breakfast was odd. "BETRAYAL" was the word on my chair. What an understatement, I thought. It was quiet around the table, maybe because of the gloomy day. Eating my oatmeal, I surveyed the table as I did most mornings to see who was still here and who was new. Our group was about half men and half women this morning. I hadn't met any of the men. The twins the women were fussing over yesterday were still here, and the others were new.

I'm pretty comfortable around most men, as long as they don't make any sleazy remarks about me. I'm most comfortable around my husband. He's the best. I'm kind of quiet around my dad and brothers and don't socialize with them often.

I looked at Jamie, smiling as she ate her food and moving her head side to side like a child. She's oblivious to her surroundings, yet there's something about her that's appealing. I actually found myself drawn to her.

The other three women I had not met: Sarah in her faint cream blouse, Brandy in a very nice blue denim-colored turtleneck, and Angela, who was sporting a yellow button-down sweater.

I used to feel threatened by some women, especially those I didn't know who were pretty with nice figures. Sometimes, when I discern a woman is a kind, decent person, I don't feel so threatened. But then there are those who look down on me or are phony or won't let me get close, and I immediately back far away.

I continued my assessment of those at the table and discovered a sixth man. I thought there were five guys, five women, and me. Where did he come from? From Day One, there had been eleven of us plus Mr. Kripling.

This gentleman – and he did seem like a real gentleman – seemed so proverbial that it was difficult for me to pull my eyes away. When I looked at him, I could have sworn I heard him speak, but he didn't open his mouth.

Now I'm hallucinating, I thought. This whole betrayal thing must have really rattled my brain.

Looking more intently, a distinct voice spoke to me, "Michelle, it is I, Jesus."

My heart skipped a beat. No one else seemed to even notice He was there. Suddenly being face to face with Jesus was unsettling, to say the least. The problem was I didn't fully trust Him. I loved Him, but it was difficult to fully trust Him when I feared something bad would happen and I'd be disappointed again.

I wasn't mad at Jesus, but because He was not moving in my husband's or my life like I wanted Him to, I felt like He wasn't coming through for us. Sometimes, I honestly believed He was never going to make a change in our circumstances. I really wanted God to prove me wrong. And I felt bad for feeling this way. I wanted everything in my life to change, from where I lived to how I reacted to people. I was tired of feeling second class, and I thought God was to blame.

Mustering up the courage to interact, my thoughts traveled to Him. "You tell me I'm first class, but I don't feel like it. I never feel special. I feel I'm a constant disappointment to You because I get angry with You. Are You mad at us? Is that why You don't bless us? Is it because of my attitude?"

Rather than hear an answer, I was startled to see Jesus' beautiful face turn to a white, pasty Mary.

What just happened? Here I was pouring out my heart, thinking I was communing with Jesus, and Mary pops up. Did she hear my thoughts like Jesus could?

This was embarrassing. How could I let myself become so vulnerable? Once again I felt betrayed. Mary had no expression on her face. With relief, I satisfied myself that she could not hear my thoughts. Only Jesus could.

However, I still blamed her for taking those books, including mine. At that moment, defeat poured into my soul. I became a slave to ease and the status quo rather than fight for what was mine.

Hidden!

###

Everyone began leaving the table, but all I could do was sit there, frozen by defeat. Even Mary slipped out of her chair and slithered quietly away.

A figure was standing next to me, and looking up, I saw Sarah. I couldn't help but notice the stunning cream blouse she had on.

"I really like your blouse."

"I'm not so sure I like it anymore," she said. "It used to be this brilliant white, and now it's this soft, faded cream color."

Not clear on how I knew this or why I was sharing it, I began to explain why her blouse was no longer white.

"You need healing! Your blouse's turning cream is an outward expression of what's happening inwardly. It will never become darker or more vivid like the other colors. Instead, as you take hold of your healing and allow the healing to change you, it will become more iridescent."

A smile came over her face; her white teeth were bright against her red lips.

"How do you know that?"

"I don't know how I know. I just do. Don't you ever know things about people or situations you can't explain?"

"No."

I didn't know what to say because I thought everyone had that type of knowledge.

"I've never heard of anything like that. Tell me more. What else do you know about me?"

Uncertain of my footing, I decided to play along.

"The more you blame God for the loss and trauma you have experienced, the more you lose power over your life and who you choose to be. This loss of power leads to a type of fatherlessness and feeling of abandonment. Over time, you have developed your survival defense mode. When it kicks in, it's game over! You are defeated. This usually happens when you're not in control of situations or when you play out scenarios in your mind about how something might transpire. You think you can predict how circumstances will work out and what the consequences will be, but you can't. These constant battles in your mind prevent you from moving forward.

You have become a defiant, stubborn, and un-teachable person whose mindset is: 'Nobody understands me or what I'm going through.'"

She sat down in the chair next to me, and I wasn't sure how she was going to react.

"How do you know what I went through and what I need healing from?"

"Because I recognize the symptoms. I've gone through the same thing. You're not the only one here who repeatedly gets beaten up by her husband or has a daily barrage of hurtful words fired at her – words, by the way, you choose to believe."

"That's incredible. What you're saying is all true, but what do I do? How do I get out of this relationship? You don't know how bad it is."

"It doesn't matter how bad it is. It's poison to your soul, and you need to leave. Don't allow him to control you. Don't allow your situation to disable you. Take control of the situation and quit walking in defeat."

"It's not that easy."

"I didn't say it was going to be easy, but it will be a journey worth taking."

"What if you're wrong? What if I'm right and there is no way out?"

"There you go playing the 'what if' tape. Did you know the number one addiction in the world is the need to be right? It's so powerful that you sabotage the healing process just to be right. In return, your state of mind is justified."

Looking at the floor, Sarah slumped in her chair. I was not sure how my next question would go over with her, but I had to ask it.

"Sarah, do you have a relationship with Jesus?"

As she raised her head, I noticed the tears welling up in her eyes. "I used to."

"Losing sight of the love of God causes us to turn to self. But God's love brings freedom."

"God can't possibly love me. If He did, He wouldn't allow this abuse to happen."

"God's not allowing this to happen, you are."

That didn't sit well with her.

"Wait a minute, I'm the victim here. You make it seem like I'm asking for the abuse, that I somehow deserve it."

"I never said that. Yes, you are a victim. But do you want to continue to be a victim?"

"What?"

"Do you want to continue to be a victim?"

"I, I never thought about it like that. I guess I didn't think I had a choice."

"We always have a choice. You chose to be in the relationship. What if you choose not to be in the relationship any longer?"

"I don't know what my boyfriend would do."

"Why does that matter? He's abusing you because you're allowing it. If you're not there for him to abuse, then what?"

"Oh, it's not that bad. He always says he's sorry."

"Really? You're going to go there. Did you hear what you just said?"

"There are some good times."

"What's the least abusive thing he's done to you?"

"Umm. The least abusive? I can handle the words he uses, like when he calls me stupid."

"Let me get this straight. When he calls you stupid, it's okay because it doesn't feel all that bad and only hurts a little. Is that what you're saying?"

"No, it hurts a lot because I'm not stupid."

"Do you feel better when he says he's sorry for calling you stupid?"

I could tell Sarah was thinking really hard about this question. That showed me she wasn't shutting down and we were getting somewhere.

"Not really, I think it makes him feel better though."

"You think he feels better when he says he's sorry?"

"Uh-huh, yep."

"Then if the least abusive act he does is very painful, and he only apologizes to make himself feel better, then please tell me what's not so bad and why you want to stay with him."

She hung her head again, and I could tell she was no longer able to hold back the tears.

"Because it's all I deserve."

Now my heart was breaking, and I began to cry. Reaching over, I pulled her close and held her as she sobbed uncontrollably in my arms. After what seemed to be at least fifteen or twenty minutes of cleansing her heart, I began to speak again.

"When we allow lies to infiltrate our heart, it changes our mindset. This hijacks God's will and purpose for our lives, causing us to become disempowered. God is ambushing your heart right now. He wants to bring the truth back into focus, giving you the power to choose a better life."

As I continued to embrace Sarah, it warmed my own heart to see her cream sweater glistening.

"Continue to let the healing resonate within you and don't believe the lies of those who try to degrade you. You are wonderfully made. God doesn't have a junk drawer because He doesn't make junk."

Sarah pulled away from me. Her countenance now matched her sweater, and she nodded her head up and down.

"Thank you! I feel like a huge weight has been lifted from my heart. It's true what you said. Everyone has a choice, and we can choose to stay in our situations and make excuses or blame others for where we are, or we can choose to do something about it."

I watched her walk away and slip out the back door. Interesting how the outdoors seemed to call all our names!

After the refreshing meeting with Sarah, I got up from the dining table and headed to my room. It felt really good to talk to Sarah and help her work through the lies she believed. I went to the window to see if I could spot her somewhere outside. Scanning the grounds, I realized I hadn't been outside in awhile and had forgotten how breathtaking it was.

I could see the maze that eluded me earlier, and near the exit from the maze, I saw people. Did they find their way through the maze, I wondered? Knowing that someone else had navigated their way through gave me hope that I could, too.

As I watched them playing, I realized I knew those people. It was Kris, Lisa and Jill. Oh, my gosh! They came to see me. I was so excited, I began to yell.

"Kris, Kris, I'm here."

They continued playing some sort of game that I couldn't make out because I was too far away.

"Lisa, Jill, Mommy's here."

I saw Lisa stop and look around for a moment, but then I heard Jill tell Lisa it was her turn at the game they were playing. Devastated, I continued watching to see if there was another way to get to them. But the maze was the only way.

I stared at the maze. So many dead ends; I could never find my way out by myself. If Kris knew the way out, why didn't he come back and show me. If he would just call my name, I could follow his voice and find my way out. I slid down to the floor and began to get upset with Kris for not helping me.

CHAPTER 13

Entitlement

As the sun set, I couldn't imagine why Kris wouldn't show me the way through the maze. I resented being stuck in this place with nobody to show me how to get out. Why did others get to leave? Everything good always happens to everyone else. I'm so sick of watching good things pass me by. I sat there for a few more minutes pondering what permitted others to receive blessings and not me.

Everyone would soon be coming together to share. I really didn't want to face Mr. Kripling or Mary, but I did want to see how Sarah and Jamie were doing. So I got up and headed back downstairs. Sarah was just coming back inside. How fun for her. She already looked so much different than this morning. Why didn't that happen to me?

We all seemed to be heading to the dining table at exactly the same time. I came to "CONTEMPT" and sat down.

The servants were on top of it tonight. Almost at the precise moment we took our seats, a bowl of soup was placed in front of each of us. Even though we didn't have any say in what we ate, the food was delicious.

Tonight we began with broccoli cheese soup. Jill didn't like broccoli, and I smiled at the thought of the face she would make when she had to eat it.

Everyone must have been really hungry because they were all eating without any conversation. Finally, when the main course of chicken Marsala was served, Mr. Kripling broke the silence.

"Strange weather we're having today. Did anyone enjoy the unusual cloudy day?"

Is he trying to trap us into admitting we went outside? I wondered. Then I remembered Jamie's mentioning she knew nothing of the rule prohibiting it. Mary obviously had misled me into thinking we weren't meant to venture outside, another reason to be angry with her.

Just then I heard a familiar voice say, in a tone that was dazzling,

"I did. It was a beautiful day, and I seemed to be able to think better. I almost made it all the way through the maze, but then it began to get dark and I came back here."

It was Sarah. She had been in the maze? I didn't think we were allowed to go in the maze. After all, it was outside, and here she was talking all about it.

Then Mr. Kripling caught me totally off guard. "Why didn't you simply keep going, Sarah. Why did you turn back?"

"It was getting dark, and I started to get scared. I felt like it would take me longer to find my way out than it would to find my way back."

"Well, at least you tried."

Well, at least you tried. Please, that was a cop-out. I try stuff all the time that doesn't work. I never get kudos for trying. I scarfed down the rest of my meal and sat while my patience ran thin waiting for the others to finish. When it came time to share, Mr. Kripling gestured for me to begin.

"I have suffered many losses because I haven't been able to be spontaneous and unashamed of my physical and emotional responses to life. I settle for second best or average in many areas of my life. I always had the potential but never the confidence to pursue greatness.

"I still allow myself to get only to a certain point before I stop. I wouldn't know how to act if I accomplished something wonderful. My friendships could have been healthier, and I could have allowed myself to express myself much more freely. I feel I've lost my childhood."

Mr. Kripling then looked at Mary but spoke to me.

"Is that why you think you have a right to certain things?"

As I looked over the writing in my book, I pondered the question. "No. I don't think I am entitled. I think I just read that I'm afraid of success."

"What I heard is you don't want to work for greatness. You are somehow entitled to it."

"Where did you get that?"

Now looking at me, he asked a delicate question. "Do you think you are entitled to something I have?"

Did he want me to reveal that I knew he and Mary had my book? He's not supposed to know this. Nor is he supposed to expose it.

"If I thought you had something of mine, yes, I would think you should give it back."

"Instead of your being upset that I may have something you think belongs to you, what if you came and obtained it all on your own?"

"Wouldn't that be stealing?"

"It depends on how you acquired it. Instead of sitting there pouting, waiting for a handout, try acquiring it without experiencing resentment."

I had to think about this one. I supposed he was correct. Nobody should feel like anyone owes them anything. While the rest of the crew shared, I explored my attitude of entitlement. At the end of the night, I sort of felt like I had been zapped with a stun gun. I seemed to have started out strong and then faded.

My sleep that night was restless. I dreamed about my youngest brother, the only person in my family with whom I am close. When he was a little boy, he often cried in his sleep, and yet on some nights sleep came easily to him.

I awoke from this dream and lay in my dark room thinking. What did any of what was going on in this place have to do with my brother? I hadn't seen him in a long time – not since his wife divorced him and moved to another state. He was ruined by that one event. He started gambling, drinking, and engaging in any self-destructive activity he could find. Kris and I didn't really want him around because of the lifestyle he was leading.

I closed my eyes and went back to sleep, re-entering the same dream. I was looking into our home when we were little. I could see my older brother coming into my room as my youngest brother slept peacefully.

On the nights my older brother did not come into my room, he entered our youngest brother's room and did the same things to him that he had done to me. Those were the nights my youngest brother's sleep was agitated. In the dream, I could hear my little brother say, "I'm sorry, Michelle, but I hope he's in your room tonight."

Then I was able to see him on the nights he appeared to be sleeping soundly, and I saw his eyes were open and he wasn't sleeping at all.

He knew what was happening to me. The turmoil was all over his face.

There was no peace in my home, apparently not for anyone. I bolted awake. I had never suspected anything was happening to my little brother as well as to me. We were merely children, but our innocence had been completely stolen from us.

I actually felt worse for him, being a boy and feeling that he couldn't protect himself, let alone protect me. What helplessness he must have suffered.

No wonder he took the divorce so hard. He couldn't bear to experience that helplessness again.

And yet, rather than try to understand his pain, we rejected him. My heart went out to him. My prejudgment of him haunted me.

It was still early, but I decided to get out of bed and have a little talk with God.

"I forgive anyone who ever has wronged me or hurt me or cursed me or lied to me, and I bless them in the name of Jesus Christ.

"Jesus, I ask You to forgive me for my failure to forgive others and for any bitterness, anger, animosity, and resentment that I have in my heart toward anyone. Forgive me for prejudging others. I see now more than ever how that gets in the way of experiencing truly great people. In Jesus' name, Amen."

I opened my eyes and saw that my room was glowing with color. The duvet on my bed was brighter than it had ever been. The curtains and even my pajamas appeared to be glowing, which caused the room to be bright.

But, though the room seemed cheery, something still was missing. I was getting ready for the day when I saw a new outfit draped over the chair: a pair of blue jeans and burgundy sweater. I made my bed and got dressed. The clothes fit perfectly, but they didn't feel like they were mine. Or, I should say, I didn't feel like me in the clothes. I headed downstairs with no intention of sneaking into breakfast this morning.

It was quite early, and I decided that instead of having to take the last chair available, I could choose which one I would sit in this morning.

As I skipped down the stairs, my pleasant new attitude was immediately stripped from me when I saw the white owl. Mary! I had dubbed her the White Owl because her large dark eyes appeared even larger against her pale complexion and completely white attire. She didn't see me, but simply getting a glimpse of her caused me to feel defeated. It was as if a thin layer of slime covered every inch of my skin. I could not shake it.

I continued to the dining table, and, though all the chairs were empty, I was drawn only to one. POWERLESSNESS! I pulled the chair out and sat down. On the table sat two silver tea sets, one with a coffee pot and one with hot water for tea. The fruit tray was assorted like something you would see in a magazine. It looked fake because it was placed so precisely. The place settings were perfect as well.

The others began to arrive at the table. Jamie put a smile on my face as she bounced to her chair swinging her braids from side to side. I wonder if she ever thought anymore about her book. Everyone began eating without waiting for Mr. Kripling. I thought that perhaps they knew something I didn't.

All the same people were at the table this morning, which I thought might mean there had not been progress. I actually liked seeing new people, and having the previous ones gone. Sarah looked really cute. Her hair was in big curls, and her blouse seemed to radiate different colors depending on the angle. She was smiling as she engaged in conversation with Brandy. Maybe it was my imagination, but every now and then, they would glance in my direction.

Mr. Kripling finally entered and looked at me with a grin that reminded me of the Grinch when he had a malicious idea. The tone in his voice oozed with false dissatisfaction. Even though many were able to leave Vic'tim Mentala, his secret desire was that they stay, in order for him to feel needed.

"I'm surprised to see you in this chair today. I was expecting so much more from you by now. We were going to have our share time tonight, but we'll move it to this morning instead."

Something about Mr. Kripling was different this morning. His tone no longer soothed my ears. I couldn't put my finger on it, but I knew I wanted to keep an eye on him to see if he changed like the rest of us. Although his clothing stayed black and white, his face and countenance were surely different today. He looked my way with that wry smile and spoke the word on my chair as if it pleased him.

"POWERLESSNESS, you may begin."

The word stung like an arrow striking my heart.

"I learned that my mind goes blank whenever something requires a difficult answer or thought process. I was surprised that I shut down and couldn't think of what to say because I never have a problem talking. I was also surprised that I don't know who I am or where I came from, therefore I cannot find my way into my future."

The others shared, and I watched Mr. Kripling, who had his hands folded under his chin.

No matter what was shared, that Cheshire cat smile never left his face. When all were done, I really wanted to be alone. I did not want to meet anyone new, contend with Mary, or even chat with Jamie. But before I could steal away, I heard my name called.

"Michelle."

Could I keep going and pretend like I didn't hear anything?

"Michelle, wait up."

I could hear footsteps running toward me as I picked up my pace. But there was no retreating. Brandy caught up to me and grabbed my shoulder. "Michelle, please."

I turned around to see Brandy in a beautiful light teal dress.

"Will you do for me what you did for Sarah?"

"Excuse me?"

"Sarah told me how much you helped her yesterday. Look at her. Can't you see the impact you had on her?"

Honestly, yes, I did see that she looked really good. But it hadn't crossed my mind that I had anything to do with it.

"Sure, why not, after all, we are expected to meet someone new every day right?"

Brandy smiled with relief and suggested we go into the den. My first thought was to rummage through the desk drawer and find my book. I couldn't do that with Brandy sitting right there, though, so I put the thought out of my mind and sat down on the couch with her.

"What is it that I can help you with?"

"I'm not sure. There seems to be so much that I don't know where to start. I have such self-hatred and I lack the ability to forgive others, and those things become intertwined and I don't know how to untangle them."

"I have to ask you, Brandy, do you believe in God."

"Yes, of course."

"No, I mean do you have a relationship with Him. Do you go to church? Do you have other believers with whom you hang out?"

"Yes, actually, I just started going to church; that's when I ended up here."

Wow! That sounded familiar.

"Then do you believe in the devil? Because some people don't realize that he is our adversary, our enemy."

"Well, sure, I don't know much about him, but I know he's real, and I've heard stories that he can make you do things you don't necessarily want to do."

"That's what I want to talk to you about. The enemy cannot make you do anything you don't want to do. God always gives us a way out, but first we have to submit to Him.

"Resist the devil and then he will not bother you anymore. You see, the enemy wants you to think he has power over you, but he only has as much power as you give him."

"Is that why I'm here because of the power I've given him?"

"That's not a bad assumption. You see you were not born by accident. You were born for a reason. We all were. Every person ever born has a purpose and a plan."

"What's my plan?"

"I'm not sure. What are you passionate about?"

"What am I passionate about? I don't know. Nothing!"

"At one time in your life, you were passionate about something, Brandy. Think back. Was there ever a time that you thought you really enjoyed doing . . . fill in the blank?"

Brandy sat there with an empty look on her face struggling to remember. I waited patiently. I could tell she was getting antsy because the room was silent. Finally, after what seemed to be at least twenty minutes, her face changed and a twinkle came into her eyes.

"There was something, a long time ago. I had forgotten all about it. My grandmother used to have a garden, and I loved planting the herbs and vegetables and learning about how she made home remedies for wounds and stomach aches and different things like that. It was so interesting how certain smells could make you feel happier or calmer. It was an amazing time for me."

"Wow! Where is your grandma now?"

"She died last year, but what I thought at the time to be odd, now sort of makes sense. She left me her book with all her remedies, and on the inscription she wrote, 'For my dearest Brandy, you're the only one who will know what to do with them.' I never knew what she meant by that."

"If you truly love doing that, you should educate yourself more about it and use it to start a business and help people."

"You think so? You think I could actually make a living doing something I love?"

"The strategy of the enemy is to seize God's purpose and His will for your life by implanting lies into your mind and, as a result, altering your mindset. We constantly battle in the mind and that's how he takes us prisoner.

"The trick is to not entertain those thoughts and to set your mind on the truth. God brought your grandma into your life to teach you what you're passionate about. She recognized it in you because she was passionate about the same thing. Then along came the cares of life and you lost your passion, so much so that you even forgot about it.

"But it's time to resurrect it and bring it back. You obviously have the gift of healing. You have the power to help many people."

"I, I never thought of it like that," Brandy said. "I have to admit I really hate my job. I work as an administrator in a hospital, and I've always wanted to do more for the patients. I even considered going to nursing school, but I can't stand the sight of blood so I gave up the idea. This is truly amazing. Now I can help the patients in a whole different way. I am so excited!"

As Brandy was speaking, her light teal sweater became a much darker shade, and her countenance lit up. I was so happy for her.

"Thank you, Michelle. Sarah was right; you do know how to empower people."

She gave me a big hug and virtually floated out of the study. What she said was very interesting. I empowered people.

The noise outside the study signaled that everyone was coming in for dinner. It seemed like the days were passing by much faster. The book would have to wait for now. I joined the others and immediately bumped into Jamie.

"Hi Jamie, how's your day going?"

With a childlike giggle, she blurted out, "Really good!"

"Really? Any particular reason?"

"I found my book."

"That is good. Where?"

"I must have overlooked it because when I woke up this morning and came downstairs, I happened to glance in the study and saw something on the couch. There it was, right where I thought I had left it."

"Really! Where is it now?"

"In my room. I can't tell you where because I don't want anyone to find it. It's pretty special, you know?"

"Yes, yes, I know, Jamie. You are truly special!"

We all headed into the kitchen for dinner because tonight was a very informal buffet-style dinner. I was pretty hungry because Brandy and I had missed lunch. I made a point to get behind Sarah so I could see how her day went.

"Hi, Sarah."

"Hi, Michelle. Did you get a chance to talk with Brandy? I know she really wanted to meet you?"

"Yes, actually I did. How was your day?"

"It wasn't bad. I wanted to go outside again and have another go at the maze, but Mr. Kripling stopped me and wanted to talk with me, so we spent most the day chatting."

"Oh, how did that go?"

"It was good. He told me that I was welcome to stay here as long as I liked and that he understood my family puts a lot of responsibility on me. He said that if he could help with that in any way, he would be happy to."

"I see." Boy, did I see. It was as if a veil had been removed from my eyes. This place was beginning to make sense for the first time. Everything here is done for us. We have fresh clothes every morning and evening; our meals are prepared, served, and taken away. There are people to befriend. We really don't have to do too much for ourselves.

Mr. Kripling seems extremely helpful, but he is also careful not to assist too much. It's also very clear that Mary has made Vic'tim Mentala her home, attempting to sabotage anyone's progress. Them failing somehow makes her feel more valuable. Mr. Kripling isn't teaming up with her, but definitely feeds off of the fact that she is so needy. He is ambivalent about anyone's success that comes through these doors. Although, he genuinely enjoys their achievements, it does become a threat to him facilitating his own self worth by enabling others.

I sat down on the stool in the kitchen and planned my next step. I was determined to get my book back, and I was going to do it tonight. I had a feeling that my book was not going to simply turn up like Jamie's did.

For some reason, I felt like I was in a battle for this book. It seemed to represent my life.

Was that it? Was I fighting for my life? *My* life! Not what someone else was dictating but what I was created to do.

After my talk with Brandy today, I realized that some, if not all, of what I had said to her also rang true for me.

So I dared to ask myself the same question I had asked her: "Michelle, what's your passion?"

I knew what I enjoyed doing. But could I? Did I have the courage to dare attempt such a thing as risky as that?

With a glance out of the corner of my right eye, I saw Mary. As if she were reading my mind, she looked at me and shook her head back and forth.

Then my thoughts came out of my mouth. "NO?"

Mary appeared shocked to have been challenged.

"Are you talking to me?"

"Yes, why are you shaking your head back and forth at me? What are you saying no to?"

"I'm just eating, Michelle. Chill out."

It's funny how people will play little games with you, but when you confront them, they suddenly retreat and pretend they weren't doing anything to begin with. That was it. I knew what I had to do, and tonight was the night I was going to do it.

CHAPTER 14

False Humility

Since share time had occurred that morning, and Mr. Kripling was gone, we were destined for an early night. I finished my meal and with a casual stride, headed back to my room. I needed time to assess the past events, and, to be honest, I had to work up the courage to make my move.

It was a lot colder than previous nights. When I entered my room, I found, much to my surprise, that the previously unused fireplace was lit. The smell of the burning wood had that distinct pleasant smell, and the warmth immediately soothed the goose bumps on my skin. The light from the fire caused shadows to dance on the wall. A pleasant feeling came over me as I saw the thick flannel pajamas on my bed. The bottoms were pink and turquoise plaid, and the top was a solid fuchsia. I took the pillows from my bed and placed them on the reclining chair in front of the fireplace.

The atmosphere was so comfortable that I just lay there mesmerized by the fire. Forgetting all the events of the day, I floated off to sleep.

A cold breeze from outside woke me in the dark room. For a split second, I couldn't remember where I was. The fire had long gone out, and I was quite cold. I looked around, but it was difficult to see by moonlight. I listened for a moment to the quiet sound of night.

Okay, I had to do this, and I had to do it now before I lost my nerve. I pulled on a pair of socks and took a deep breath.

I left my room and crept down the hallway. At the top of the stairs, I realized I had never before been out of my room at night. How was I going to see in the dark? During the day, natural sunlight lit the place.

Slowly I walked down the stairs, listening. The lifeless night was so still and quiet it was eerie. As I got closer to the bottom of the stairs, my eyes began to adjust to the darkness. Much to my surprise, I could see the whole downstairs from the moonlight streaming through the windows.

The air was heavy. Perhaps it was the intensity of the moment, but it felt ghostly. With careful abandon, I found my way to the den. Happy to find the door open, I tiptoed inside.

The moonlight touched only the entryway inside the French doors leading to the porch outside, causing the rest of the room to be much darker. Feeling my way around, I located what I was looking for - the desk with the books in it.

But how was I going to find evidence of Mary taking the books in this dark room? I resolved to leave Mary to herself. That was no longer my mission. Ever so carefully, I slid open the desk drawer inch by inch, not making a sound. I could make out the books inside. There seemed to be about five.

Not knowing which one was mine, I thought about taking them all. I rationalized that I would discover who they belonged to and return them to their rightful owners.

Click! The table lamp next to the couch came on. Someone was there. My heart stopped for a moment. The person obviously had been there the whole time, waiting for the precise moment to catch me in the act.

Not sure whether to turn around and not knowing who I would see, I stood frozen. Then a very familiar voice said, "Why not take it back?"

Turning only my head, fear gripped me as I saw Mr. Kripling sitting on the couch.

"Ummm, what?" was all that came from my mouth.

"The book, why not take it back?"

I couldn't believe my ears. He was admitting he knew the books were stolen but didn't seem to care. He said again, "It's your book, take it!"

Still in a state of shock, I couldn't speak. How had he known I would be coming? I hadn't seen him since this morning, and I hadn't known myself I was coming until that evening at dinner. Mr. Kripling persisted.

"Are you or are you not going to take your book?"

"Can I? I mean, you don't mind?"

It had never occurred to me that it would be acceptable to simply come in here without sneaking around and take the book back.

"Why would I mind?"

"Well, you knew that Mary took it and yet you didn't do anything about it, so I thought you didn't want me to have it."

"What was I expected to do to Mary for taking the book?"

"I don't know, punish her."

"Punish her?"

When he repeated my words, they sounded silly. In fact, I sounded downright childish. In that moment, I felt like I was the one in the wrong, not Mary. I looked down at the books in the drawer and immediately spotted mine. It was the only one titled, *"WHO YOU CHOOSE TO BE."*

"Michelle?"

"All right, she doesn't need to be punished. It was a stupid thought."

"You have two choices, Michelle. You can take your book, take responsibility and quit blaming others for where you are in your life, or . . ."

I waited for the alternative, but he said nothing else. Instead, out of my mouth came, "Or not."

I saw that he was right. A victim mentality had not only crippled me but also my relationships with my family, friends,

221

and, most of all, God. It was as if I'd been on an automated walkway, never stopping to get off as I watched life go by.

I picked up the book, closed the drawer, turned the lamp off and left Mr. Kripling in the dark.

It was still dark out, but finding my way to the stairs was easier now that I no longer felt the need to be sneaky. With newfound self-assurance, I scurried up the stairs to my room. The room was even colder than when I left. There was still plenty of wood, so I made a fire. The flames got bigger, and comforting warmth filled the room. I lay on the bed holding my book close to my chest. I turned out the light and fell into a sweet sleep.

I awakened to a brilliant morning. Thankfully the fire was still burning. I took my book with me into the bathroom because I was determined not to be careless with it again. The hot shower flowed over my tired muscles as I relaxed and let thoughts of Mary wash away. Today was the first day of the rest of my life.

So much seemed different. For one, my clothes were the same blue cargo jeans and burgundy sweater I had worn yesterday. I usually have a fresh change of clothes waiting for me. Not wanting to stay in my pajamas, I put them on. Only this time, they seemed very comfortable. Not because I wore them the day before, but because I knew them somehow, they seemed to belong to me.

By now the fire was dwindling. I made up my bright and colorful bed with a light spirit, knowing I had slept there for the last time. I stuck my book in the side pocket of my jeans and went downstairs. No one was around yet, so I decided to help myself to some breakfast. The thought of my traipsing through the dark the night before made me giggle.

I sat at the island in the kitchen and was almost finished with my oatmeal when Angela walked in, startling me.

"Whoa, what are you doing here?" I asked.

"Are you being sarcastic?"

"No, no, I mean, I couldn't find anyone and thought I might be alone. Do you know where everyone went?"

"Yes. Sarah talked them into going outside to conquer the maze. I swear the girl is obsessed with that thing."

"Why didn't you go?"

"What's the point? Everyone sees people on the other side of the maze, and they keep shouting to them for help in finding their way through the maze. How crazy is that?"

"I don't understand. It makes perfect sense to me. Those on the other side of the maze must have found a way through it."

"Not necessarily."

Angela started making herself a sandwich as she explained her theory.

"The way I see it, they couldn't tell us how to get through the maze because they were never on this side of the maze in the first place."

I became a little distracted with her green olives and cream cheese on dark rye sandwich.

"Is that good?"

"Yeah, you want to try a bite?"

"Sure." Even in that little gesture, I could tell there was something different inside me. Before, even if I wanted to try something offered, I would decline thinking that was the more humble choice.

"Wow! That's not bad at all. Matter of fact, it's pretty good."

"My dad use to make it for me all the time when I was little."

Suddenly, the castle became alive again as everyone began to saunter back in from their adventure in the maze. As I pondered Angela's theory, I thought that would explain why Kris and the girls weren't able to help me through. They didn't know the way because they had not been here before.

I looked back at Angela and noticed that she was wearing black skinny jeans and a cute silver top. Everyone began to pile into the kitchen. I could clearly see how pale the colors they wore were compared to Angela's and mine. I thought to myself that I wanted to get to know her better. There was something very appealing about her.

Intruding on my thoughts, Mr. Kripling came in with the others, filthy and laughing. I spotted Jamie giggling as well. I asked, "What happened to him?"

"Oh he was out there helping us get through the maze, and when he summoned us back inside for lunch, he slipped on a patch of mud and down he went."

I couldn't help but smile at the thought. But why would he be helping them get through the maze? It never occurred to me that he wouldn't know the way out. I wondered how long he had lived in the castle and how many countless people he must have encountered.

He was such a nice man, always wanting to help everyone. Doing everything for them. We didn't really have to do anything for ourselves because he had most everything covered. No wonder some people stayed. Then I remembered the other books in the desk drawer in the den. I could pick mine out easily because the others were blank. They had nothing written on them.

Sadness swept over me for these lost ones who couldn't find their way out.

Mr. Kripling, still laughing about his unfortunate fall, motioned us all into the dining room. "Get your lunch and bring it in here; we are going to have our share time."

In the afternoon? That was a first.

Angela was just finishing her sandwich. We both grabbed a banana and an orange and headed for the dining room. I gravitated toward the chair that read "REPENTANCE." Of course, no matter where I sat at the table, Mr. Kripling always motioned to me to lead off. This time I looked down, but there was no book. There was no script. Nothing to go on but what I had experienced in that place. I stood up for the first time and began to speak unaided.

"Victim mentality is actually a false humility. Self-worth is true humility. Choosing to be a victim gives strength to insecurity and inferiority. It has made me blind and allowed me to only partially appreciate an abundant mindset and my self worth. So many people know the truth in their hearts but choose to live where they are familiar no matter how poisonous it may be. We have lost sight of the love of God and turned to self, choosing the familiar over freedom. God's love brings freedom."

Sitting down, I wasn't sure how anyone would react. I began to hear a lone clap. Normally, it would have been followed by more clapping but not today. I looked over and saw Angela, the only person clapping.

Then it became unmistakably clear – she was not clapping to rally the others but was genuinely applauding my efforts.

"Thank you God!" I whispered.

CHAPTER 15

Bold Love

The castle was quiet. I was walking out to the grand living room where I had seen the old couple a few days earlier when someone came alongside me and slipped her arm through mine. I was surprised to see Angela.

"Hey, girl, whatcha doin'?" she asked.

"I'm not sure. I hadn't really spent much time in here and I wanted to see what it was like."

In silence, we stared out the oversized bay window that overlooked the courtyard in front of the castle. Somehow we seemed connected, like kindred spirits. It was a refreshing feeling compared with days past. I was the first to break the silence.

"Have you sat in all the chairs at the table?"

"Yep."

"What do you think will happen next?"

"Whatever I want to happen. I can either go around the mountain again or I can begin to climb."

We stood there awhile longer in silence. For the first time since I had arrived, I actually felt like I had connected with someone. And yet I had a sick feeling in my stomach because I knew that it was going to be short-lived. I could tell by the tone in Angela's voice that she was going out the front door, never to return.

"So you think those who continue to stay here want to be here?"

"What do you think, oh Enlightened One?" Though we were both staring straight ahead, I could hear the smile in her voice.

"I think that being vulnerable takes great strength and does not mean you're weak," I said. "I also think trusting takes courage."

"But first you must be committed."

"How so?"

"Commitment brings trust, which brings courage and confidence in God. Very few people take control over what they are committed to. Spouses aren't committed to each other; employees and employers aren't committed to each other; family members aren't even committed to each other."

Angela went on as if she were remembering a time in her past and, perhaps, decided to make a change for her future.

"People will mostly commit to something as long as it's convenient. Even then it gets difficult to keep their commitment. Even something small, like our agreeing to meet somewhere at a certain time. If I'm a half hour late, that means I wasn't committed to meeting with you.

"Most people conduct themselves as if breaking such a small commitment is not only okay, but normal. What people don't realize is that my tardiness conveys to you that something else was more important than me keeping my word. People are subsequently casual with each other, and casualness breeds casualties. When I keep a commitment, it conveys value to the person or cause I'm committed to and it creates self-worth."

I had never realized how powerful it was to build healthy relationships. When people feel valued, they walk with a new sense of confidence.

We watched the sky turn a picturesque pink and orange as the sun set, and then we parted ways. Angela headed toward the front door.

I didn't want to say goodbye, but I hoped we would meet again some day. I retreated in the other direction to my room. Reaching the top of the stairs, I thought: "Why didn't you go with her?"

Why didn't I go with her? I didn't know that was an option. After all, I still have one more chair. Then I remembered Angela's answer when I asked her what happens next.

"Whatever I want to happen."

Could it be that simple? Could I honestly choose to do something without worrying what others might think of my choice? I went in the room and sat on the floor next to the bed and pulled my knees into my chest. I asked God to give me clarity.

"God, remove the things that obstruct my view of who You are and all that You have available to me. I agree to have freedom from all limitations. Forgive me for looking to people to celebrate me, and when they did not, growing weak and allowing the opinions of others to limit me. Things that have pursued me in the past will no longer rule my life. What I focus on, I empower.

Give me a deeper understanding of You and Your Kingdom."

I sat for awhile pondering the last chair. "BOLD LOVE!" Something fell out of the side pocket of my pants. It was my book. I picked it up, got up and walked over to the window. I looked again at the title, "*WHO YOU CHOOSE TO BE,*" and carefully opened the book. This time there wasn't only writing but photographs. They definitely were not of my past. Perhaps they were photos of my present. I didn't recognize them. I saw many known and unknown faces. Was this my future? I continued to turn the pages and ponder the scenes before me.

Looking at those pages took me back to the words Jamie spoke the first day I was here, "We can stay here as long as we like." I was no longer interested in the book. I decided, in that moment, that I no longer wanted to be here. As I stood up with a mindset to follow Angela's lead, something came over me. "Was that courage?" Could it really be? I stood to my feet with a new resign to walk out that front door and leave this place behind.

Before I could process what was happening, I ran down the stairs, past the kitchen, through the living room and straight out the front door. The door did not hesitate to slam right behind me. It was clear to me now, there was no going back, only forward. I stood there contemplating my next move when I felt someone come from behind and put their arms around my waste.

"Kris."

I turned around and gave him a joyous kiss. Then he stopped and gave me a long-awaited, heartfelt embrace. I still couldn't fathom what was happening.

"Where have you been? How did you get here?"

"What do you mean? I've been here all along. I never left."

It was he, not the servants, who had left all those wonderful treats in my room. But in this place I couldn't recognize the value people were setting before me. I couldn't accept or acknowledge such a thing.

As Kris spoke, all that was before me transformed. I looked from one place to another. The castle was gone, replaced by our little three-bedroom home. I felt like I had just come through a space/time continuum.

"Kris, I need to understand something. I was in this place. It was a large white castle called Vic'tim Mentala, and others were there with me. What happened?"

"Honey, yes, having a victim mentality can be largely where you live every day, and there are many who live right there with you."

"Victim mentality. I never thought of it like that."

"Most people who have a victim mentality don't realize it. That's a part of being rendered powerless."

"But it was so real. There was a guy that sort of ran the place, Mr. Kripling. He seemed to have everything in order, so we didn't really have to do anything."

"That makes sense."

"What do you mean?"

"When someone has a victim mentality, they allow an enabler into their life. That way they don't have to take responsibility." This was starting to become irritating. Kris seemed to have an answer for everything.

"There was also an evil woman named Mary who stole my book and lied to me about our not being able to go outside.

"But every time I accused Mary of doing something wrong, I sounded so juvenile."

"All right, now you're starting to sound like a victim again."

He was right. It was true what I said about Mary, but I had chosen to believe her. And when she tried to steal my life, I grew more determined, stronger, and no longer made excuses.

"I do need a different perspective on opposition. Mary was evil, but her antagonism helped me overcome and become a better person."

We sat down on the front porch. Kris beamed as he looked at me. "You look different. I'm so proud of you for coming out of that. Tell me, did you ever remember your passion?"

A car pulled into the driveway and two grown women resembling Lisa and Jill got out. They had to be at least nineteen and twenty-four years old.

"Hey, Mom. Hi, Dad."

I ran over and gave both of them a tight squeeze.

"Is everything okay, Mom?"
"Yep, everything is perfect."

###

We all walked into the house, and I couldn't help but feel remorse for having allowed my past to rule my future as the years blindly passed by. I was so wrapped up in what I should have that I forgot to be grateful for what I did have.

Kris and I put our arms around each other's waists, and I shared my feelings of regret with him. "They grew up so fast. I missed it."

"We were both in a bad place," he said. "But there's so much more to come. Let's be present in every moment and embrace it. Agreed?"

"Agreed! And yes, about my passion? I did find it. I will begin writing again. I promise."

We all went into the kitchen, and I became captivated by my tremendous family interacting with one another in such a playful manner.

"What's for dinner, Mom?"
Some things never change.

"I'm not sure. Let me see what we have to make."

Looking through the refrigerator was such a small task. But the thought of having the opportunity to make my family dinner sent a tremendous wave of satisfaction through me.

I was pulling lettuce, tomatoes, and cheese out of the refrigerator when the phone rang. My hands were full, and even though nobody was in any hurry to answer the phone, it didn't bother me. I had a choice of how to react.

"Could someone get the phone please? My hands are full."

Lisa ran to the kitchen. "Sorry, Mom, I didn't realize you were tied up."

In that instant, I grasped just how much my actions affected others as well as the atmosphere around me.

"Hello."

"Is this Michelle?"

"No, this is Lisa."

Lisa's face turned pale as she listened to whoever was on the other end of the phone.

"What is it, sweetie? Who is it?"

She looked at me and pointed the phone toward me.

"It's someone named Cassie asking for you. She says she's my aunt."

My heart dropped as I took the phone with great hesitation. The only thought rushing through my mind was that Lisa's dad, Adam, had found me. I took a deep breath and thought to myself, "Michelle, you can do this; you're not that person anymore. You don't have to do anything you don't want to do. The nightmare is over." Lisa had a curious look on her face as she handed me the phone.

"Mom, are you all right?"

"I will be in a minute."

I calmed my heart and took the phone. It was time to conquer this.

"Hello?"

"Michelle, is that you? It's me, Cassie?"

Her voice sounded just as I remembered it all those years ago.

"Oh my gosh. How are you?"

What was really running through my mind was what does she want?

"I'm great. I can't believe I finally found you."

"What's going on, Cassie?"

"I felt like I needed to find you. I'm Cassie Katrell now. About six months after you left, I couldn't handle it anymore. You were always my strength. You were the one who helped me keep my sanity. I finally realized that if you could leave, I could leave, too. With some help from my dad's friends, I left and hid out in Reno, Nevada where I made a home for me and the kids and got remarried."

"I had no idea that I had such an impact on you. Thank you so much for sharing. What happened after you left? Did Joe try to find you?"

We were talking like we had never been apart. It was so nice to hear her voice.

"Of course, he came looking for me. It took about eight years. By then, I was dating the man I would marry. I was getting the kids in the car for school when I saw this man coming toward me. I didn't even recognize him until he got close.

"When I realized what was happening, the old fear gripped me. He looked horrible, Michelle. His eyes were yellow and so was his skin. I got the kids out of the car and quickly back to the apartment and called the police.

When Joe saw the police, he got in his car to leave and – would you believe it – they pulled him over for drunk driving. It was 7:00 in the morning, and he was drunk.

"Within a few months, I found out why he looked so awful. He was dying of cirrhosis of the liver."

"You're kidding."

"No, his mom phoned me when he was on his death bed wanting me to come because he was calling for me."

"Did you go?"

"Absolutely not. I couldn't believe she had the nerve to ask."

"How did she find you?"

"I had phoned her when Joe came by and told her to keep him away from me. Next thing I knew, he was dead."

"Wow, crazy!"

"It gets crazier. Adam took Joe's death really hard and went on a drinking binge, drinking everything in sight, even cough syrup.

"A year later, he ended up with leukemia and died. Their Grandma had died right after Joe did, and Grandpa couldn't handle it. He put a gun to his head."

My guard was completely down by now. It was my long lost Cassie, no more terror, just my dear friend.

"That must have been so difficult for their mother, losing both her sons and her parents."

"I work in a hospital and have access to certain records. I put in the mom's name, and a death certificate came up. She died of cancer also about a year ago. The only one alive is the dad, left behind all alone."

"They all died such horrible deaths," I said. "It's strange seeing all the pain they caused coming back on them."

"Yeah, we give the term survivor a whole new meaning."

"No kidding. It's so good to hear your voice."

Over the course of a week, Cassie and I had many phone conversations and caught up on the last fifteen years or so. I booked a flight for Lisa and me to go to Reno so she could meet her cousins.

At the airport, Cassie and I embraced like school girls, smiling with tears rolling down our cheeks. It wasn't until that moment that I realized how much Cassie was a part of me. We were not simply ex-in-laws; we were sisters.

Lisa and I also met Cassie's daughter from her new marriage. It was music to my ears when the twelve-year old greeted me with a hug and called me auntie.

A grownup Joe Jr. and a young woman who used to be Baby Carrie were waiting for us when we arrived at the house. Lisa became fast friends with her newfound cousins. As Cassie and I watched them interact, we couldn't help but notice how much Lisa and Carrie were alike.

"Cassie, I have to ask you. Why after all these years did you choose now to contact me?"

"I tried to find you several times but came up empty. I figured you had remarried and had a new name, so I began to look for Lisa. I knew if I found her, I could find you.

A few months ago I became a believer in Jesus Christ. I became a Christian, Michelle. When I had that experience, something within told me I had to find you. Now I know why. You're obviously a believer, too."

"Wow! That's pretty powerful. How awesome is God."

As the weeks turned into months, Cassie's crew and mine became one big family. Cassie and I talked practically every day and planned trips to visit each other.

It became clear to me that Cassie was brought back into my life so I could help her work through the terror of her past. With much prayer and inner healing, Cassie was able to avoid Vic'tim Mentala.

AFTERWORD

What the colors symbolize:
    Orange=Hope
    Yellow=Purification
    Pink=Right relationships
    Cream=Healing
    Silver=Strength
    Green=Healing
    Blue=Authority
    White=Victory

So many times we think we are living in victory, and we are really living in victim. Living in victim can be quite deceiving.

Define who the enabler is in your life. Just as Mr. Kripling made life easy at Vic'tim Mentala, you have a person you run to that will justify each situation. Who is that for you? There may be more than one. It's time to move them out away from you.

Many times there are people in our lives who we would call a villain or an enemy. Whenever you're around them, they rub you the wrong way. I'm going to suggest it is not an accident they are in your lives.

Just as Mary challenged Michelle, God used Mary as fuel to empower Michelle and overcome the evil from within. She became a stronger person because of it. Michelle became armed with a purpose.

How can you use those "villains" in your life to fuel you forward into an overcomer?

It's time to take that step, just as Michelle did when she walked out the front door. It will not feel comfortable, just as the weather changed and was no longer comfortable for Michelle. But you will gain power over your old mindset and you will be able to see a clearer view of who you were created to be. You too will be armed with a purpose.

Please share with me how this book impacted you and your next step.

www.hidden.sandrafuruvald.com